The
Big Golden Book of
ANIMALS

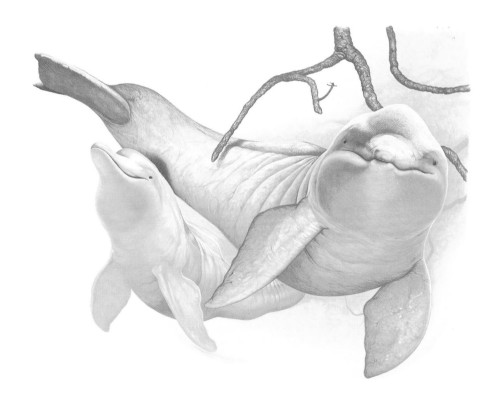

AN ILEX BOOK

Copyright © 1991 Ilex Publishers Limited

Illustrated by Martin Camm, Jim Channell, John Francis, and Dick
Twinney, courtesy of Bernard Thornton Artists

Designed by Richard Rowan and Hugh Schermuly

Created and produced by Ilex Publishers Limited
29–31 George Street, Oxford OX1 2AJ.

Color Separation by Chroma Graphics (Overseas) Pte. Ltd.
Printed in Singapore by Kim Hup Lee Printing Co. Pte. Ltd.

The
Big Golden Book of
ANIMALS
How and Where They Live

Mark Carwardine

A GOLDEN BOOK • NEW YORK
Western Publishing Company, Inc., Racine, Wisconsin 53404
All trademarks are the property of Western Publishing Company, Inc.
Library of Congress Catalog Card Number: 91-70364
ISBN: 0-307-16555-8 / ISBN: 0-307-66555-0 (lib. bdg.)
A MCMXCI

CONTENTS

RAIN FOREST ANIMALS 6

AYE-AYE 8
AMAZON RIVER DOLPHIN 10
HOWLER MONKEY 12
SLOTH 14
MALAYAN TAPIR 16

WOODLAND ANIMALS 18

GENET 20
BADGER 22
RING-TAILED LEMUR 24
BUSH BABY 26
BARN OWL 28

WATER ANIMALS 30

FISHING CAT 32
GAVIAL 34
HIPPOPOTAMUS 36
MOOSE 38
TORRENT DUCK 40

GRASSLAND ANIMALS 42

CHIMPANZEE 44
SPOTTED HYENA 46
AARDVARK 48
BAT-EARED FOX 50

MOUNTAIN ANIMALS   52

SNOW LEOPARD   54
GORILLA   56
CONDOR   58
JAPANESE MACAQUE   60

POLAR ANIMALS   62

NARWHAL   64
EMPEROR PENGUIN   66
POLAR BEAR   68
ARCTIC HARE   70

SEA ANIMALS   72

MARINE IGUANA   74
CALIFORNIA SEA LION   76
SHARK   78
BLUE WHALE   80
SEA OTTER   82

DESERT ANIMALS   84

RATTLESNAKE   86
SCORPION   88
BANDED MONGOOSE   90
CAMEL   92
AUSTRALIAN FRILLED LIZARD   94

INDEX   96

RAIN FOREST ANIMAL

Nowhere else in the world is there a greater variety of animals and plants than in the tropical rain forests, or "jungles" as we sometimes call them. From the highest treetop to the darkest forest floor, the rain forests are alive with jaguars, gorillas, gibbons, tapirs, toucans, frogs, butterflies, and hundreds of thousands of other creatures.

There are many different kinds of rain forest, including tangled mangrove swamps along the coast, steamy jungles in the lowlands, and mountain or "cloud" forests in the uplands. Most are found near the equator, in South America, Africa, and Southeast Asia. But rain forests are disappearing rapidly as people cut and burn them down.

**Toucan
South America**

Toucans are best known for their enormous beaks. They may use them to frighten off their enemies.

The male proboscis monkey's enormous nose may hang over its mouth.

The male quetzal's tail feathers often grow to as much as two feet in length.

**Proboscis monkey
Southeast Asia**

**Quetzal
Central America**

**Vampire bat
American tropics**

**Gibbon
Southeast Asia**

**Golden lion tamarin
South America**

**Jaguar
Central and South
America**

Vampire bats, which live in Central and South America, feed on the blood of other animals.

Gibbons spend nearly all their lives in the trees, rarely coming down to the ground.

The golden lion tamarin is one of the rarest of all the monkeys and apes. Fewer than one hundred live in the wild.

Jaguars are rare because so many have been killed for their attractive fur coats.

7

AYE-AYE

ENDANGERED
This bizarre animal may soon become extinct as nearly all of the forests of Madagascar where it lives have been cleared.

The aye-aye has such huge ears that it can hear the slightest sounds in its rain forest home.

Aye-ayes can hang upside down from branches, using the strong claws on their feet as hooks. This leaves their hands free for feeding or cleaning.

The aye-aye looks like a creature from outer space. It has ratlike teeth, a bushy, squirrel-like tail, a catlike body, and huge eyes and ears. In fact, for more than one hundred years scientists tried to classify it.

Aye-ayes are extremely rare. They live in some of the rain forests on the east coast of Madagascar and are active only at night. The daytime is spent sleeping in ball-shaped nests made of leaves and branches. As soon as the sun goes down they wake up and start moving around.

Aye-ayes travel through the trees easily and jump about like lemurs and monkeys. They even hang upside down, using their claws as hooks to cling to branches.

Their favorite food is grubs that live under the bark of trees. The aye-aye carefully places one of its ears next to the bark and listens for the slightest sounds of the tiny animals. Then it quickly gnaws a hole into the tree and pulls out the grubs with its long, thin middle finger, which looks like a bent twig. Most aye-ayes make grunting noises when they are eating.

If you get too close to one of these strange animals, it hisses or makes a "ha-hay" call by blowing through its nose. This is given only as a warning to frighten off intruders, but most human tribes in Madagascar are scared by the noise.

The aye-aye uses its long, thin middle finger to pull out grubs hiding underneath the bark of a tree. It also uses this strange, twiglike finger for combing its hair and for scratching.

Aye-aye fact file:

The aye-aye is about the size of a pet cat, and its bushy tail is at least as long as its body.

At one time, the tiny island of Nosy Mangabe, off the coast of Madagascar, was thought to be the only place in the world where aye-ayes lived. But in recent years many more of these rare animals have been found in the rain forests of the mainland.

The aye-aye sometimes eats coconuts. It gnaws a hole in the side, then dips its middle finger into the coconut milk, and pulls it out to suck.

AMAZON RIVER DOLPHI

ENDANGERED
River dolphins were once common in many regions of the Amazon. Now they are threatened with extinction. The main causes are mercury pollution released into rivers by gold miners and the construction of dams. Both make it difficult for the dolphins to find enough healthy fish to eat.

Amazon river dolphins are very friendly animals. They often come to the aid of injured or troubled companions, even risking danger to themselves. They have been seen swimming one on either side of an injured dolphin, carrying it to the surface to breathe.

Amazon river dolphins spend most of their time underwater and come to the surface to breathe for only a few seconds at a time. Unlike many other dolphins, they never leap out of the water.

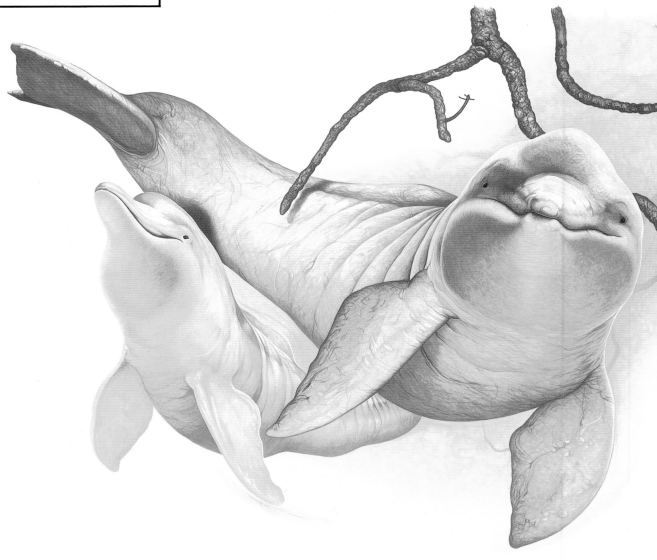

River dolphins have very small eyes capable only of telling the difference between day and night.

Little more than six feet long, Amazon river dolphins are very brightly colored compared with most other members of the dolphin family. The older they are, the pinker they become.

In some parts of the Amazon Basin, where they live, the dolphins even help the local people. They come to the call of the fishermen and herd fish from deeper water into their nets in the shallows.

They often live in pairs, hunting together mainly for fish but sometimes for crabs and shrimps that they swallow whole. Baby river dolphins, or calves, are thought to be born between July and September. They are almost half as long as their parents but continue to grow for many years. Like their parents, they have very poor eyesight. They use a form of echo-location – similar to that of bats – to find their way around and to catch food.

Dolphin fact file:
There are five different kinds of river dolphin, named after the rivers in which they live: the Amazon, the Ganges, the Indus, the Yangtze and the La Plata.

There are thirty-seven different dolphins altogether.

Dolphins range in size from the tiny Heaveside's dolphin, little more than three feet long, to the famous killer whale that grows to as much as thirty feet in length.

Dolphins have large brains and are very intelligent animals.

HOWLER MONKEY

Monkey fact file:
There are more than one hundred and thirty species of monkey around the world, including tamarins, macaques, baboons, and capuchins.

Howler monkeys are excellent climbers and spend most of their time high in the treetops.

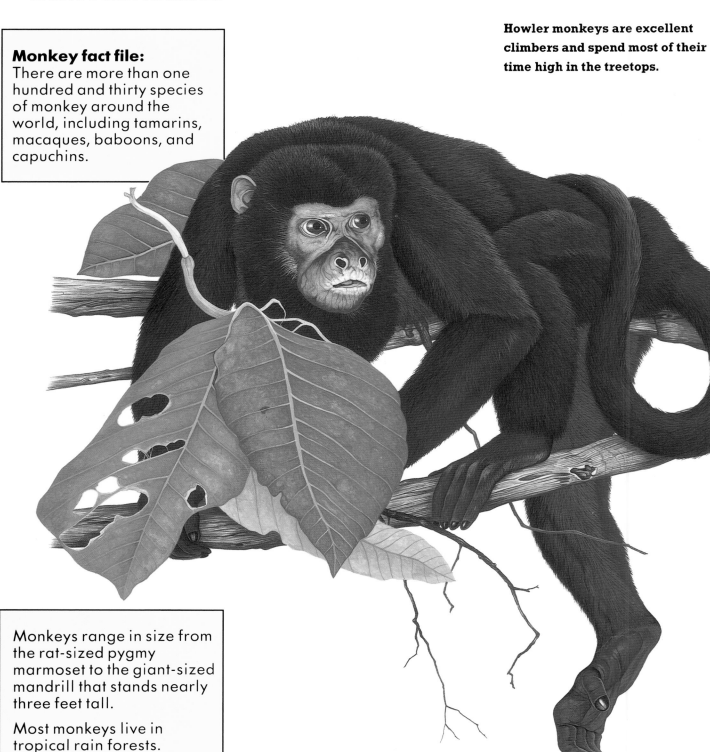

Monkeys range in size from the rat-sized pygmy marmoset to the giant-sized mandrill that stands nearly three feet tall.

Most monkeys live in tropical rain forests.

12

In the huge trees of South America's rain forests lives the noisiest monkey in the world, the howler monkey. Its cries and howls can be heard up to three miles away. The sound, rather like a lion's roar, helps to keep other howler monkeys, in neighboring groups, away from their favorite trees.

Usually about ten howler monkeys live together, though sometimes there may be as many as fifty in a single group. They spend a great deal of the day and all of the night resting. But whenever they feel hungry, they get up and move around to look for food – mostly leaves and fruit. Although they sleep in places nearer the ground, they move up the trees to near the roof of the jungle early every morning. Then they sing and start the day's work of finding food.

Howler monkeys have very long and flexible tails that serve as extra arms, even allowing them to hang from branches upside down. This is useful because their hands and feet are then free for eating. In fact, their tails are so strong that if the monkeys make a mistake when climbing and fall, they can use them to catch a branch on the way down. This is why very few howler monkeys that fall actually hit the ground.

> ### *ENDANGERED*
> *The forest homes of howler monkeys are being destroyed and replaced with farms, cattle ranches, and plantations. The monkeys are also hunted for their meat, sometimes even in protected areas.*

Howler monkeys often use their strong tails to hang from branches and then eat leaves and fruit while they are upside down.

SLOTH

Sloths have long, stiff hair all over their bodies, making them very rough to touch.

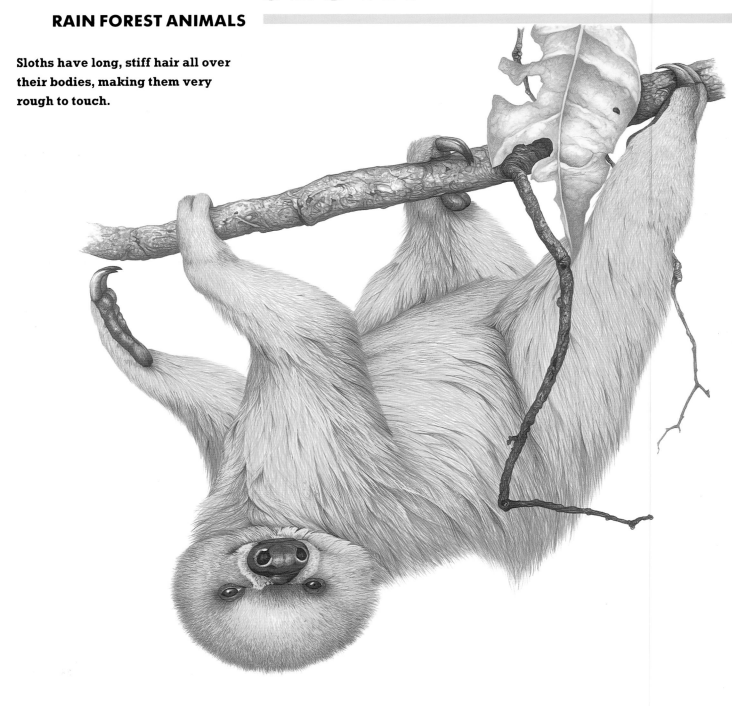

Sloths spend nearly all their lives hanging upside down from branches. Sometimes they even remain attached after they have died. They are incredibly slow and inactive animals, moving at a snail's pace and sleeping some fifteen hours every day.

Sloths live high up in the jungle trees of tropical Central and South America. They are most "active" at night, when they feed on leaves, shoots, and fruit, but they can occasionally be seen during the day. In the sunlight, their coats often look green because tiny plants, called algae, grow on the hairs. The green helps to camouflage the animals in the trees.

Although sloths are very slow, they are able to defend themselves against jaguars, ocelots, and other predators with their sharp teeth and claws. The curved claws, which can reach almost four inches in length, are mostly used for hanging onto branches but, in a fight, can inflict severe wounds.

Sloths are good swimmers and can cover long distances using the crawl or breast stroke. Walking, however, is almost impossible. Their long claws get in the way, and their legs are so weak that they have to pull themselves along slowly with their front feet, dragging their bellies along the ground.

> **Sloth fact file:**
> There are five different kinds of sloth.
>
> Some sloths have three fingers on each hand, others have only two. But they all have three toes on each foot.
>
> Sloths make two different noises: a high-pitched whistling and an unpleasant hissing.
>
> Sloths live as long as twelve years in the wild.

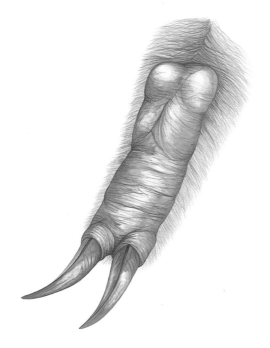

Sloths use their sharp curved claws to defend themselves against predators and to cling to branches. They spend their entire lives upside down, even sleeping, eating, mating, and giving birth in that position.

15

MALAYAN TAPIR

Living in the tropics, tapirs spend a great deal of time wallowing in shallow water, trying to keep cool.

Tapir fact file:
There are four different kinds of tapir, living in Central and South America and in Southeast Asia.

Tapirs have rather poor eyesight and rely much more on their excellent sense of smell and good hearing.

Big cats, such as jaguars, leopards, and tigers, are the main predators of tapirs.

Tapirs rarely walk in a straight line. They prefer a zigzag course through the jungle.

In parts of Southeast Asia, an unusual animal can sometimes be seen walking through the jungle with its long nose close to the ground. It is the rare Malayan tapir, carefully sniffing its path to make sure it is on the right trail.

The tapir also uses its nose as an extra finger to pull food within easy reach of its mouth: It feeds on grasses, water plants, soft twigs, leaves, buds, fruits, and green shoots. These are mostly eaten at night in forest clearings and along riverbanks.

Its dramatic black-and-white coloring makes the Malayan tapir difficult to see in the dark.

16

There is a legend that says the Malayan tapir was once completely black but wore a white blanket over its back to keep warm. As a result, it is sometimes still called the blanket tapir.

Actually, tapirs spend a great deal of their time trying to keep cool. They are excellent swimmers and often rest in water during the heat of the day. They have even been seen holding their breath and walking along the bottom of rivers, just like hippos.

Baby tapirs look quite different from their parents. They have brown coats, dappled with white spots and stripes, which provide good camouflage for hiding in jungle undergrowth. By the time they are six months old, however, they have the same black-and-white coats as their parents.

> ### *ENDANGERED*
> *This rare jungle animal has become endangered because the rain forests have been cut down. With its home destroyed, the tapir has retreated to remote mountain regions. The Malayan tapir is now protected by law and can be found in most large forest reserves in Southeast Asia.*

The tapir looks rather like a cross between a pig and an elephant, but it is more closely related to the horse and the rhinoceros.

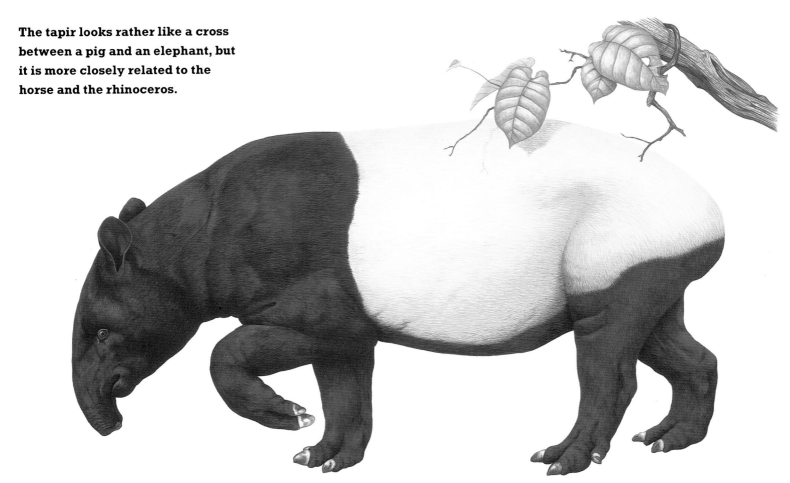

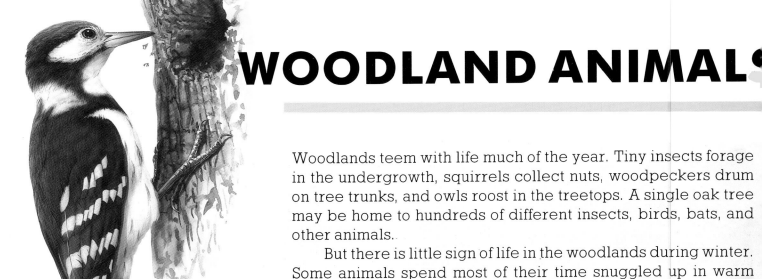

WOODLAND ANIMALS

Woodlands teem with life much of the year. Tiny insects forage in the undergrowth, squirrels collect nuts, woodpeckers drum on tree trunks, and owls roost in the treetops. A single oak tree may be home to hundreds of different insects, birds, bats, and other animals.

But there is little sign of life in the woodlands during winter. Some animals spend most of their time snuggled up in warm underground burrows or in holes in the trees. They emerge only occasionally to look for food. Others disappear altogether. Many birds, for example, migrate to warmer countries. Other animals – like hedgehogs and woodchucks – hibernate until the following spring.

Woodpecker
Europe, North Africa, Asia

The woodpecker makes a hole in a tree in which to lay its eggs.

The red fox is common in towns and cities as well as woodlands.

Chipmunks spend most of their lives collecting food, eating, and sleeping.

Raccoons will eat almost anything. They are often found raiding garbage cans.

Raccoon
North America

Red fox
Temperate Northern Hemisphere

Chipmunk
North America

**flying squirrel
Asia**

**Koala
Australia**

**Eurasian
red squirrel**

**Mynah birds
Asia**

European brown bear

European polecat

Mynahs are famous for copying
other sounds. They can even mimic
a closing door or a ringing
telephone.

The flying squirrel glides through
the air, using the skin between its
arms and legs as wings.

Red squirrels feed mostly on seeds
from pine cones.

Koalas are excellent climbers but
have difficulty moving on the
ground.

The European brown bear feeds on
grasses, berries, and small
mammals.

The European polecat uses its
excellent senses of smell and
hearing to hunt at night.

GENET

Genets are difficult to see in the wild because they are very shy and come out only at night. Their spotted fur makes them almost invisible.

In the Middle Ages, before people had pet cats, genets were very popular animals that were often kept as rat catchers in many parts of Europe. They look a lot like cats, but they are much slimmer and have shorter legs. They are, in fact, related to the mongoose (see pages 90–91).

There are several different species of genet. Most live in Africa, but one is also found in the Middle East and southern Europe. They are difficult to see as they are shy animals, only coming out at night. They sleep by day, curled up in a hollow tree, under a bush, or in tall grass where their spotted fur blends in with the surroundings, making them almost invisible. To let other genets know they are around, however, they mark their paths with their scent.

Silent and stealthy hunters, genets usually travel alone or in pairs. They search the forests for insects, fruit, and birds, happily climbing around in the trees. On the ground, they forage for lizards, snakes, mice, and rats. They sometimes catch frogs, bats, and other small animals.

Young genets are born in a hollow tree or burrow, in nests lined with vegetation. They are blind at birth, but their eyes open after about eight days. They soon begin to venture from the nest and finally leave home after about a year.

> **Genet fact file:**
> Genets are found mainly in Africa and also in parts of the Middle East and southern Europe.
>
> Some genets have several different names. For example, the aquatic genet is also known as the Congo water civet.
>
> Genets normally live about twenty years in the wild, but one captive animal lived for thirty-four years.

Genets sometimes wrap themselves up in their long, bushy tails to keep warm while they sleep.

BADGER

The European badger's favorite food is earthworms. It can catch and eat several hundred in just a few hours. If the ground is very dry, however, and there are not many earthworms to be found, it also eats rabbits, voles, slugs, nuts, berries, and other foods. The American badger feeds almost exclusively on rodents.

Badgers spend the daytime sleeping underground. A typical badger burrow is a jungle of tunnels and rooms. It has many entrances and may be used by ten or more of the animals. The rooms, or chambers, are lined with heaps of bedding, consisting mostly of leaves and grass that the badgers drag in on dry nights. They often spring-clean by replacing old bedding with new. Some badger burrows are hundreds of years old, having been used by many generations of badgers.

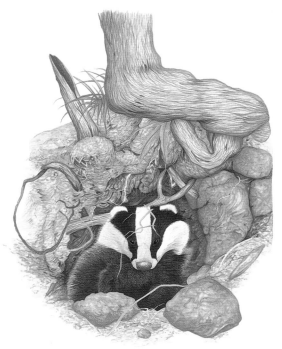

On a good night a European badger can catch several hundred earthworms within a few hours.

Badgers have a really good scratch every evening because of the annoying fleas and lice that live in their fur.

The badgers emerge cautiously from their burrows at dusk or during the night. At first, they sniff the air for signs of danger, then stand outside one of the holes to have a good scratch. Occasionally, in remoter areas, they come out earlier and can be seen in broad daylight. Most people, however, sight them at night in the beam of a car's headlights as they amble across the road.

All badgers have long claws and powerful front legs. They are known for their speed in digging. Like other members of the weasel family, they give off a musky odor when disturbed.

Badger fact file:
There are nine species of badger. They live in many parts of North America, Europe, Africa, and Asia.

Not all badgers are black and white. The stink badger of Borneo is streaked with brown, black, and yellow. Ferret badgers, which live in many parts of Asia, are yellowish brown.

Badgers belong to the weasel family, which includes wolverines, skunks, otters, and polecats.

On dry nights badgers collect balls of leaves and grass and take them into their burrows to sleep on.

Most of the ring-tailed lemur's day is spent foraging for food such as fruit, leaves, and occasionally insects. It takes only a short nap at midday and is sometimes active after dark as well. It often dips its tail in special scent glands on its wrists and wafts it at other lemurs during "stink fights."

ENDANGERED

The number of lemurs living on Madagascar has been getting smaller ever since human beings settled on the island. The forests have been cut and burned to make room for crops and cattle. Many lemurs have become extinct, and most of those now surviving are endangered.

Ring-tailed lemurs can leap easily from tree to tree, but they do not feel as safe, high in the air, as do other lemurs or monkeys. They prefer strong, wide branches to the slimmer, more dangerous ones their relatives often use. Best of all, they like to have their feet firmly on the ground.

Ring-tailed lemurs live in the forests and scrubby areas of southern Madagascar. They are easily recognized by the black-and-white tail, which is always held in the air in the shape of a question mark when they are walking or running along the ground. They use their tail like a flag, to show companions exactly where they are.

Up to twenty or more lemurs live together in one troop. They often purr when together, just like cats, and will even meow if separated from their friends. Other calls they make include a yap or a scream – if a dangerous animal like a snake or a hawk is nearby. Their howling call sounds something like a wolf's.

For the first week of life, the young ring-tailed lemur clings to its mother's chest. When it is a little older, it prefers to ride around on her back.

Lemur fact file:
Lemurs live mainly in the forests of Madagascar, but there are also some on the nearby Comoro Islands.

About fourteen different lemurs have already become extinct, and many of the twenty-four species alive today are endangered.

The smallest lemur in the world, the lesser mouse lemur, is only about the size of a mouse. The largest, the indri, can be over two feet long.

25

BUSH BABY

Bush babies leap from tree to tree with their arms and legs tucked tightly against their bodies.

Bush babies sleep in little nests during the day but come out at night to feed.

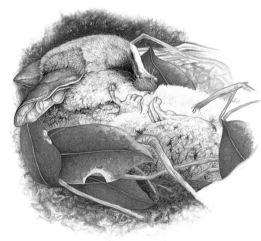

In the middle of the night, deep in the forests and shrublands of Africa, strange sounds are sometimes heard, just like human babies crying in their cribs. But these noises are actually made by bush babies, whose loud calls really do sound human.

The several species of bush baby range in size from that of a squirrel to one almost as big as a house cat. They are all expert jumpers, making flying leaps to travel from tree to tree. Each time they jump they tuck their arms and legs tightly against their bodies in midair. They can jump as far as fifteen feet in one leap. During their travels, they can cover several miles in a single night. They also have special suckers on their fingers and toes to help them cling to trees.

Bush babies have big eyes for seeing in the dark, and even the slightest sound will be picked up by the keen hearing of their large ears. But when they sleep during the day in a nest of leaves and twigs, their large ears must be folded up before they settle down.

Bush babies feed at night on tree gum, insects, lizards, mice, and small birds. At first, very young ones are "parked" on a branch while their mothers search for food. When old enough, they prefer to follow her around. However, they often have to make clicking calls for her to return or slow down because they cannot keep up.

Young bush babies like to be close to their mother and follow her wherever she goes.

Bush baby fact file:
There are six different species of bush baby, all living in Africa.

Some bush babies live in rain forests. Others live in a variety of different woodlands and even grasslands.

When bush babies are hungry, they sometimes watch for insects flying past and snatch them out of the air with their hands.

Bush babies escape from their predators by leaping and bounding away between the branches and tree trunks. Within seconds they can be more than thirty feet away.

27

BARN OWL

Barn owls have probably given rise to more scary stories than any other animal. Ghostly white in the darkness, they can often be seen in the evening and late at night in churchyards, silently flying low. They sometimes even appear to glow in the dark, and they utter unearthly screeches and wails, spooky hissing and gargling screams.

But barn owls are not particularly dangerous birds. They are welcomed by farmers because they catch pests such as rats and mice. Special trays are often placed in barns for the birds

When they are hunting, barn owls always fly with their long white legs lowered, ready to pounce.

Barn owls sometimes hunt from perches, such as fence posts or walls. They look and listen for small animals moving around in the darkness.

to nest and roost in. Found in North and South America, Europe (including western Russia), Africa, southern Asia, and Australia, they are among the best-known owls.

Barn owls hunt at night, with the help of remarkable hearing and eyesight. To a barn owl, a cloudy, moonless night probably seems no darker than a dim, overcast day does to us. They fly back and forth over fields and meadows in search of their prey. Rarely do they fly more than a few feet above the ground, except when they have to pass over higher bushes, walls, and hedges. Mice, voles, and shrews are their favorite foods. They will also catch rabbits, rats, small birds, bats, frogs, large insects, and even fish.

Owl fact file:
There are more than one hundred and thirty different kinds of owl around the world. Not all of them are active at night. Many hunt mainly during the daytime.

The largest owl in the world is the eagle-sized great gray owl. The least pygmy and elf owls are the smallest owls in the world, both sparrow-sized.

Farmers welcome barn owls because they catch rats, mice, and other farm pests. They often place special trays in their barns for the owls to use as roosts and nest sites.

WATER ANIMALS

There are many different freshwater habitats around the world. They range from tiny ponds to large lakes; from small streams to the mighty Amazon River, and from tropical swamps to coastal mudflats.

They are home to an extraordinary variety of animals. Some prefer to stay on land along the riverbanks or lakeshores, but many are strong swimmers and spend a lot of time in the water. Then there are fish and other animals that can breathe underwater and spend their entire lives in the depths.

Rivers, lakes, and marshes are also popular with people and, sadly, many are becoming polluted.

Kingfisher
Africa, Eurasia

The kingfisher dives from a perch above the water to catch fish.

Beavers live in dome-shaped lodges they build in streams and small lakes.

Manatees are also called sea cows, because they graze on underwater grasses.

Otters are excellent swimmers but are equally at home on the land.

Salmon swim against powerful river currents to reach their breeding grounds.

Beaver
North America

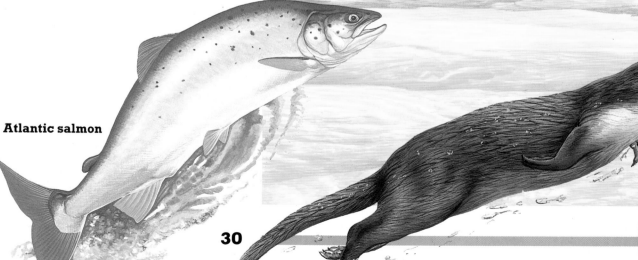

Atlantic salmon

European ot

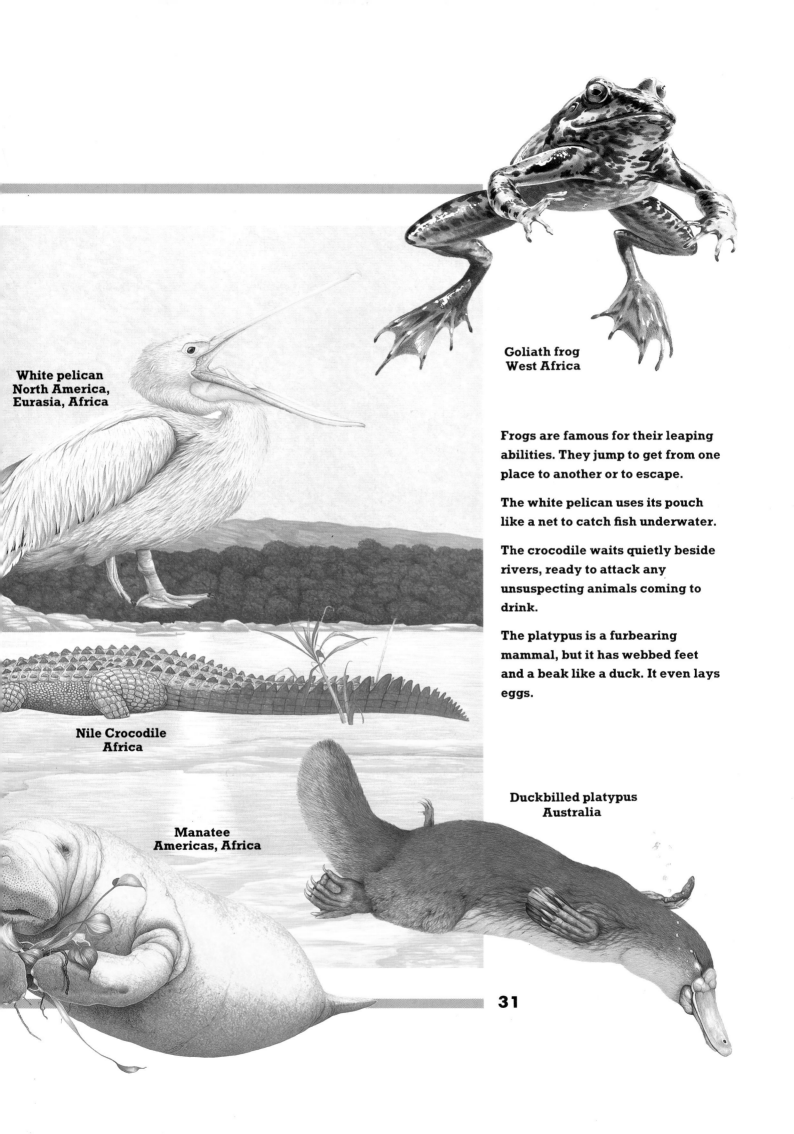

Goliath frog
West Africa

White pelican
North America,
Eurasia, Africa

Nile Crocodile
Africa

Manatee
Americas, Africa

Duckbilled platypus
Australia

Frogs are famous for their leaping abilities. They jump to get from one place to another or to escape.

The white pelican uses its pouch like a net to catch fish underwater.

The crocodile waits quietly beside rivers, ready to attack any unsuspecting animals coming to drink.

The platypus is a furbearing mammal, but it has webbed feet and a beak like a duck. It even lays eggs.

31

FISHING CAT

The fishing cat is unusual among cats because it does not mind getting its fur wet.

Most cats do not like water, but the fishing cat often spends hours paddling in rivers and lakes. It is quite happy swimming in deep water, and sometimes even dives under the surface. Its toes have slight webbing between them – just like those of a duck – to help it swim more easily.

Cat fact file:
There are thirty-five different cats around the world, ranging from the black-footed cat, only fourteen inches long, to the tiger, which can grow up to nine feet long.

Wild cats are found in most parts of the world, except Australia and New Zealand, Madagascar, the Antarctic, and certain parts of the Arctic.

The most serious threat to the survival of the world's cats is the fur trade. Many thousands of these animals are killed every year for their beautiful coats.

Fishing cats not only eat fish but also many other kinds of small animals.

Fishing cats live in many parts of Asia, including such islands as Sri Lanka, Sumatra, and Java. They make their homes in marshes, mangrove swamps, and along creeks and rivers. Every day they patiently and quietly crouch on a rock or sand-bank, waiting for a fish to swim nearby. As soon as one does, they quickly use a paw as a fishing net to scoop it up, or they pin the fish to the streambed. If they have a bad day's fishing, they also hunt for shrimp, crabs, snails, frogs, snakes, birds, and mice.

Fishing cats are considerably larger than house cats. Their fur is short and rough, and their tail is extremely thick. The kittens, born in April or May, do not grow as big as their parents until they are at least nine months old.

GAVIAL

The gavial has long rows of very sharp teeth that are used to keep a tight hold on slippery fish.

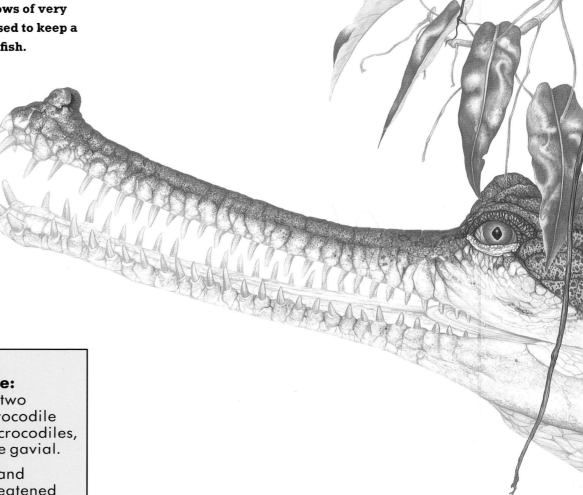

Crocodile fact file:
There are twenty-two members of the crocodile family, including crocodiles, alligators, and the gavial.

Many crocodiles and alligators are threatened with extinction because they have been killed for their skins, which are used to make handbags and shoes.

The American alligator has been known to live to nearly one hundred years old.

The largest member of the crocodile family is the saltwater crocodile, which can grow to more than twenty feet long.

Gavials sometimes keep warm by sleeping on the bottom of rivers. Odd-looking members of the crocodile family, they much prefer hot and sunny weather – when they can sunbathe all day long – to cold winds and rain.

They were once very common animals in rivers all over India, Nepal, Pakistan, and Bangladesh. But so many of them were killed by hunters that, ten years ago, only about sixty were still alive.

Special sanctuaries were therefore set up, in which they could live in safety, and their numbers are now slowly increasing. There are now several thousand of them in the wild.

Gavials dig holes in the ground in which to lay their eggs. These are usually no more than a few feet from the water's edge, as the animals find it difficult to move on land. When all the eggs have been laid, the females carefully cover them with soil. The females then return to the river and, from a safe distance, quietly watch the nests to make sure their eggs are not stolen by mongooses, lizards, or people.

Male gavials grow up to twenty feet in length; the females are generally much smaller. They hunt at night for fish, using their special piercing teeth to keep a tight hold on slippery prey. Each gavial has more than a hundred teeth in its slender mouth.

> ### *ENDANGERED*
> *Although their numbers have increased in recent years, gavials are still endangered. These crocodilians have been heavily hunted for their skins. Many have also been drowned in fishnets. A major threat to their survival is forest destruction. When forests are cut, a lot of silt then washes into the rivers. The gavial lives in the deeper parts of fast-flowing rivers, but as silt deposits build up, these soon become shallow.*

A gavial egg has a hard but fragile shell, much like that of a bird's. Once the young gavial has broken out of its shell, it grows very quickly.

HIPPOPOTAMUS

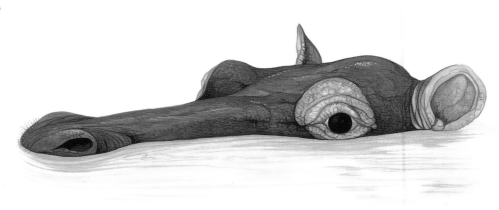

The eyes, ears, and nose of a hippo are on the top of its head. A hippo may be almost completely submerged for hours.

The hippo's unmistakable grunting and growling call makes it one of the noisiest animals in Africa. It is also one of Africa's biggest and most dangerous animals.

Hippos spend most of the day sleeping and resting in lakes and rivers. Lying in the water with just their eyes, ears, and noses visible above the surface, they do nothing more active than open their mouths to yawn. Occasionally they squabble. Fighting among hippos is common, and their long razor-sharp teeth often cause serious injuries. Fights may last for an hour or more.

Hippo fact file:

There are two kinds of hippo: the common hippopotamus and the pigmy hippopotamus.

One common hippo weighs as much as ten pigmy hippos.

In deep water, where they cannot reach the bottom, young hippos stand on their mothers' backs.

The common hippo likes to lie in the water with lots of other hippos. Sometimes there may be several hundred of them together.

Hippos' backs, however, are often used by other, daring, animals as rocks. Terrapins and young crocodiles lie on them to sunbathe; while such birds as egrets and storks use them as perches for fishing.

Hippos travel along special "hippo paths" on the bottom of rivers and lakes, walking along them like ballet dancers in slow motion. Hippos may weigh 4,000 pounds or more, and so they do not float to the surface. Normally they remain underwater for only four minutes but can stay down as long as half an hour.

Hippos become really active at night, leaving their daytime water homes and walking as much as several miles to their favorite grazing areas, or "hippo lawns." They may look clumsy on land, but they can easily run as fast as a person over short distances. A hippo may eat as much as one hundred pounds of grass and other plants every night before returning to the safety of the water in time for daybreak.

Hippos are so heavy, they can walk along special "hippo paths" on the bottom of rivers and lakes. They look like ballet dancers in slow motion.

MOOSE

Deer fact file:
There are thirty-six different species of deer around the world, including roe deer, marsh deer, reindeer muntjacs, and pudus.

The southern pudu, the smallest deer in the world, is about the size of a hare. It lives in Chile and Argentina.

All male deer (except the Chinese water deer) have antlers that are used mainly as weapons during fights over females. These antlers drop off and regrow each year. Female reindeer also have antlers, and use them in fights over food.

Moose normally walk very carefully and quietly through their woodland homes. If they come upon hunters – and see no means of escape – they will even try to hide behind a tree rather than run. But if there is a chance that they have not been seen, they risk running away as fast as they can. Some moose have been known to exceed thirty miles per hour in making an escape.

The American moose, called elk in Europe, are the largest deer in the world. With their massive antlers, they are unmistakable animals. Sometimes they stand over six feet high at the shoulders. Once found in many parts of Europe and all over the United States and Canada, they have been killed off by hunters in some regions. However, they are still common in many places and continue to be hunted for sport.

Moose sometimes wade in shallow water to feed on water plants, their favorite food.

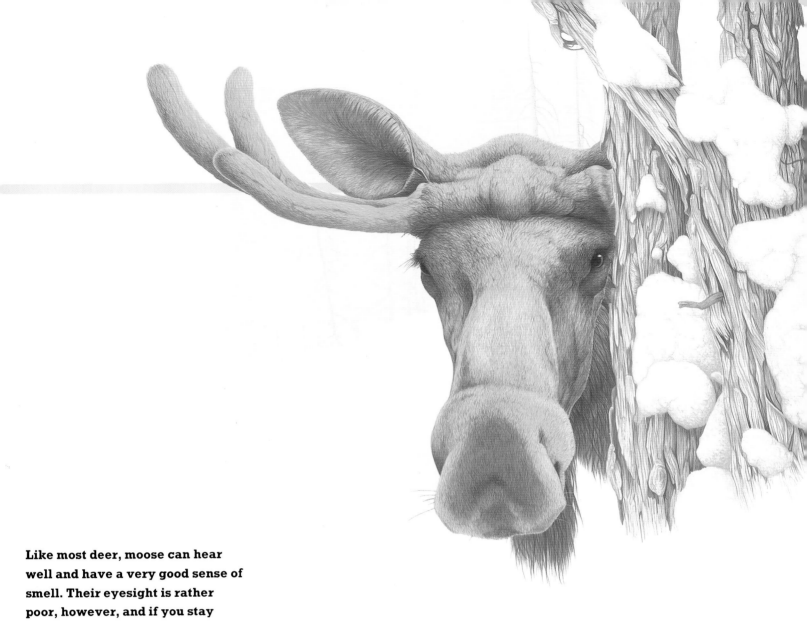

Like most deer, moose can hear well and have a very good sense of smell. Their eyesight is rather poor, however, and if you stay perfectly still, they are unlikely to see you.

Although very strong and enormous animals, moose are afraid of people and will sometimes hide behind trees to avoid being seen.

Moose are most active at dusk and dawn but can be seen almost anytime during the day. They are particularly fond of marshy regions and will paddle in the water for hours.

Water plants are among their favorite foods, and they sometimes disappear under the surface in their eagerness to find them. They also feed on twigs, the bark of trees, and on many other plants. A particularly hungry moose will eat more than a thousand plants in a day.

TORRENT DUCK

In the rivers of the Andes mountains in South America, an amazing bird spends most of its life battling the fast-flowing currents. It dives off boulders into the water and completely disappears underneath. It can fight its way upstream for half an hour or more, swimming with just its head above the surface. Sometimes it gives up, lets go, and shoots back down the river with the current, bouncing and bobbing as it goes.

This remarkable and striking bird is a torrent duck. The male has a stunning white head streaked with black; the female a beautiful reddish face and breast.

Torrent ducks show no fear of the dangerous, swirling white waters in which they spend most of their lives.

The torrent duck has a streamlined shape for swimming underwater, a long stiff tail for steering, and enormous webbed feet.

Perfectly adapted for swimming in swirling white waters, the torrent duck has a streamlined shape and a long stiff tail for steering. Its webbed feet are so enormous that torrent duck eggs have to be specially big for the baby duck's feet to fit inside before hatching. The feet are usually used for swimming, but they are also useful if the bird wants to run across the water when it is in a hurry.

Torrent ducks even have sharp claws for gripping slippery surfaces. These help the duck to keep its foothold on a submerged rock when it is resting and the water is swirling around its legs.

Torrent ducks feed only on the larvae of stone flies that live among the underwater weeds of their river homes. As a result, they never venture too far away and rarely need to fly.

Duck fact file:
There are about one hundred and forty different ducks found all over the world, except in the Antarctic.

After the breeding season, most ducks lose all their old flight feathers and are unable to fly for almost a month before the new ones grow in their place.

In most species of ducks, the males and females look very different. The males tend to be brightly colored while the females have brownish feathers and are much plainer.

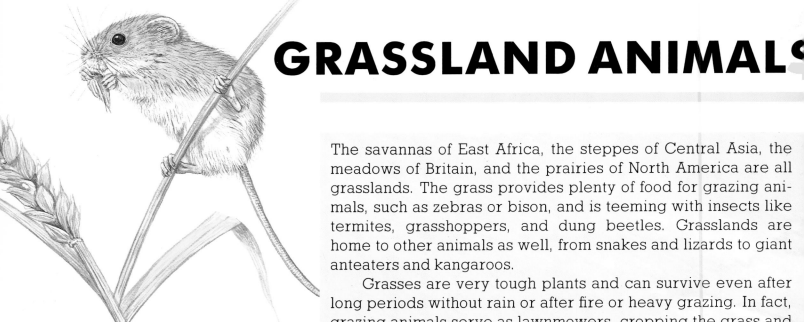

GRASSLAND ANIMALS

The savannas of East Africa, the steppes of Central Asia, the meadows of Britain, and the prairies of North America are all grasslands. The grass provides plenty of food for grazing animals, such as zebras or bison, and is teeming with insects like termites, grasshoppers, and dung beetles. Grasslands are home to other animals as well, from snakes and lizards to giant anteaters and kangaroos.

Grasses are very tough plants and can survive even after long periods without rain or after fire or heavy grazing. In fact, grazing animals serve as lawnmowers, cropping the grass and encouraging new growth.

**Harvest mouse
Eurasia**

The harvest mouse spends much of its time scrambling about in the tops of grass stems.

Large communities of prairie dogs live in underground "towns" on the prairies of North America.

Cattle egrets are often found close to zebras on the scorching-hot grasslands of Africa.

The black rhinoceros is one of the rarest animals in Africa. Fewer than three thousand five hundred of them are left in the wild.

**Black rhinoceros
Africa**

**Prairie dog
North America**

**Cattle egret and zeb
Africa**

Vulture
Africa

Red-billed quelea
Africa

Kangaroo
Australia

Giraffe
Africa

Lion
Africa, India

The red-billed quelea is the commonest bird in the world.

Vultures are ungainly birds on the ground but graceful in the air.

Some kangaroos can cover more then twenty-five feet in a single leap.

The giraffe uses its long neck to reach leaves at the top of acacia trees.

Lions sometimes hide in the long grass ready to pounce on their prey.

CHIMPANZEE

When a young chimp's mother is busy, another female in the troop will babysit for her.

ENDANGERED
Many chimps are exported for scientific research and also for the tourist trade. Hunters kill mother chimps so they can then catch their babies. In some places, these captives earn lots of money for their owners by being photographed with tourists. Chimps are also hunted for their meat.

Chimpanzees, which live in the jungles and grasslands of Africa, are very similar and closely related to people. They often hold hands when they are together. They kiss when they meet, can even smile, or look worried if something is troubling them.

They are also highly intelligent animals. Unlike most other monkeys and apes, they are able to use tools. For example, they lower sticks into ant or termite nests, wait for the insects to crawl onto the stick, then sweep them into their mouths before they have time to bite. They also use sticks or rocks to smash open fruit and hard shells, or they throw them to frighten off leopards and other enemies. They have even been known to use leaves like sponges, dipping them into water and then washing with them.

Chimpanzees eat mainly fruits, young leaves, seeds, and flowers, but they will also take honey, eggs, caterpillars, birds, and anything else they can get their hands on. On occasion, they eat small monkeys, pigs, and antelopes. They live in "chimpanzee towns" that consist of fifty or more chimps, but they usually feed and wander on their own. If one of them finds a lot of food, however, it barks excitedly to announce the good news to its friends. Then they all rush over to join in the feast, grunting softly to show their pleasure and contentment.

Although chimpanzees spend much of their time on the ground, they climb into trees to sleep after dark. Each night they build a new leafy nest in branches about thirty feet above the ground.

Chimpanzee fact file:
There are two kinds of chimpanzee: the chimp we are familiar with and the much smaller and rarer pygmy chimpanzee, or bonobo.

Chimps are big animals. When standing, a full-grown male can be as tall as a man.

Like human beings, chimps can alter the shapes of their faces to smile or to look angry, frightened, or worried.

Chimps use sticks as tools, poking them into ant or termite nests and sweeping the insects out to eat.

SPOTTED HYENA

In many parts of Africa, it is common to hear strange giggles, yells, growls, weird howling screams, and bloodcurdling laughter at night. These noises are made by the spotted, or laughing, hyena.

Hyenas are like garbage disposals on four legs. They eat almost anything, including skin, hair, bones, horns, and hooves. There is very little that their strong teeth and powerful jaws cannot crush.

The spotted hyena is about the size of a large dog. It also looks rather like a dog, but its back legs are much shorter than the front ones. Its closest relatives are thought to be mongooses and civets.

46

The spotted hyena, a powerful animal with a large head, has tough bone-crushing teeth and strong jaws that grip very tightly. This is the largest member of the hyena family.

Most of hyenas' hunting is done at dusk and during the night. During the daytime they sleep in burrows, tall grass, thick brush, or between rocks. Hyenas may travel up to fifty miles in one night's foraging, using their excellent eyesight, hearing, and smell to find food. They catch a variety of animals, including gazelles, zebras, and wildebeests, and often eat animals already killed by other predators. It is common for hyenas to chase away lions and vultures, for example, to steal their food.

Although there may be as many as eighty hyenas living together in a group called a clan, they normally split into smaller packs to hunt. A single pack can eat an entire zebra in about fifteen minutes. If there is any food left over, however, they often bury it in muddy pools. Unlike squirrels, they nearly always remember where their food is hidden.

Hyena fact file:
There are four different kinds of hyena: the aardwolf and the striped, brown, and spotted hyenas.

Hyenas never seem to tire and will happily trot around their grassland homes for hours and hours.

Hyena cubs are very playful animals and love to chase one another and splash around in water holes.

47

AARDVARK

The aardvark can dig a hole in the ground faster than several men with shovels.

As soon as it gets dark, this strange-looking animal appears on the African plains. With its piglike nose, enormous pointed ears, and worm-shaped tongue, the aardvark is quite different from any other animal in the world.

It spends the day sleeping in a burrow and emerges to feed after sunset. For several minutes it will wait cautiously at its burrow exit to test the night air for any sign of danger. But as soon as it is sure the coast is clear, it will dash off in a zigzag path looking for ants and termites. It drags its tail on the ground as it runs.

Sometimes an aardvark will travel several miles in one night. When it eventually finds an insect nest, the hungry animal quickly digs into the sunbaked earth with its powerful feet and strong claws.

The aardvark has a long, sticky tongue used to lick up termites and ants.

Then it sticks its nose into the hole and licks up the ants or termites with a long, sticky tongue. Tough skin protects the aardvark from being bitten, but it has to close its nostrils to prevent the insects from crawling up its nose!

Aardvarks are very timid animals. If frightened, they bleat loudly and run back to their burrows as fast as they can, or they may even dig another burrow with amazing speed. But if necessary, they can fight off attackers, like leopards and wild dogs, often by turning a somersault and giving their unfortunate attacker a hard kick as they land.

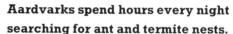

Aardvarks spend hours every night searching for ant and termite nests.

Aardvark fact file:
Aardvarks are sometimes known as earth pigs, bush pigs, or ant bears, though they are related to neither pigs nor bears.

Aardvarks eat mostly ants during the dry season and termites during the wet season.

Since they have a very good sense of smell, aardvarks always walk around with their noses close to the ground.

BAT-EARED FOX

GRASSLAND ANIMALS

Bat-eared foxes prefer insects to any other kind of food.

The bat-eared fox has such enormous ears that it can hear insects moving in the grass. It spends hours listening for the rustling of termites and dung beetles, its favorite foods. Although the fox sometimes eats mice, young birds, and even scorpions, it is the only member of the dog family to prefer insects over any other kind of food.

Bat-eared foxes live in eastern and southern Africa. During the hottest part of the day in the dry grasslands, their ears also act as radiators, enabling the animals to lose heat.

Bat-eared foxes sleep curled up like cats, with their tails over their eyes.

The bat-eared fox got its name from its enormous ears.

They spend most of the day in underground dens (which they dig themselves) or in.the enlarged burrows of other animals. These often have many entrances, and chambers with many yards of tunnels.

As soon as the sun sets they emerge to wander in search of food. Mostly they hunt near herds of zebras and wildebeest, where dung beetles and other insects are particularly common.

Young bat-eared foxes spend the first three or four months of their lives underground before leaving the safety of their dens to begin foraging with their parents. Dwarfed by their ears at first, they grow to full size when about six months old.

Fox fact file:
There are twenty-one species of fox around the world, found in North and South America, Europe, Africa, and Asia.

Foxes live in a wide variety of habitats, from the Arctic tundra to the center of cities.

Foxes belong to the dog family, and they are related to wolves, coyotes, jackals, and domestic dogs.

51

MOUNTAIN ANIMAL

Volcano rabbit
Mexico

Mountains are formed over millions of years and cover almost a quarter of the world's land surface. Among the most spectacular mountain ranges are the Alps in Europe, the Andes in South America, the Rocky Mountains in North America, and the Himalayas in Asia.

The higher you climb up a mountain, the colder it gets. This change in the weather divides the mountainside into different layers, ranging from thick forests to tundra and rocks. This is why some animals prefer to live near the bottom of a mountain and others like to live near the top. But many of the snow-covered summits are too cold and windy for even the hardiest mountain animals. It is impossible for anything to live on the top of Mount Everest, for example, which is 29,028 feet tall and the highest point on Earth.

The volcano rabbit is the smallest and one of the rarest rabbits in the world.

Pikas often live on rocky mountain slopes and are always barking or bleating at one another.

The Spanish ibex is a kind of wild goat and is expert at climbing and jumping.

The giant panda is now found only in a few remote bamboo forests in southwestern China.

Giant panda
China

Pika
North America, Asia

Spanish ibex
Europe

**Chamois
Europe**

**Chinchilla
South America**

**Cougar
North, Central, and
South America**

**Llama
South American Andes**

**Yak
Central Asia**

The chinchilla's thick coat helps it to survive the cold weather of the high Andes mountains in South America.

The chamois is famous for its breathtaking leaps across mountainous terrain.

Cougars hunt alone for deer in mountain forests and many other habitats in North and South America.

Closely related to camels, llamas have been tamed by people living in the South American Andes.

Wild yaks live at higher elevations than almost any other animal. They live in the mountains of Tibet and parts of China.

SNOW LEOPARD

Leopard fact file:
There are three different leopards – the common, clouded, and snow leopards.

All leopards have spots.

Many common leopards are completely black (although their spots still show through the black fur). They are known as black panthers.

Snow leopards have as many as four cubs in a litter, though two or three is more common.

The snow leopard is an exceptionally beautiful cat with long, silky fur. It is closely related to the common leopard and is similar in size and shape. But it does not roar like other big cats, more commonly making a loud, eerie moaning call.

Snow leopards are now very rare because so many have been hunted for their attractive spotted coats. They can still be found in some of the high mountains of central Asia, where they move gracefully and easily over difficult terrain. They have even been known to jump as far as fifteen feet from one rock to another.

Snow leopards sleep at night and in the middle of the day, usually in rocky caverns or crevices in the mountains. During the early morning and late afternoon, though, they are active and roam widely looking for food. Snow leopards eat all kinds of other animals, including mountain goats, sheep, deer, wild boar, marmots, and pikas. In winter, they have to move from the high, treeless mountain slopes when their prey descend to live in the warmer forests.

Young snow leopards are born in spring or early summer. They stay hidden inside a rocky shelter lined with their mother's fur until about three months old. Then they cautiously emerge to see the outside world for the first time, always staying close by their mother's side. After about a year they leave for good and begin to wander the mountains alone in search of a new home.

Snow leopards are expert long jumpers and can leap as far as fifteen feet from one rock to another.

Little is known about the beautiful snow leopard because it is very rare and extremely shy.

ENDANGERED
There are probably only a few hundred snow leopards still in existence today. Large numbers of these beautiful cats were killed for their fur, for sport, or by farmers concerned about the leopards attacking domestic livestock. Because of the reduction of its natural food supply including mountain goats, sheep, and deer, the snow leopard has of necessity turned to domestic animals for food.

GORILLA

ENDANGERED

The mountain gorilla is one of the rarest animals in the world. Logging and cattle ranching have destroyed large areas of the gorillas' forest homes. These big animals need a lot of space in which to live and so their survival depends greatly on the conservation of their habitat.

Adult gorillas are very patient with their children and spend hours playing with them.

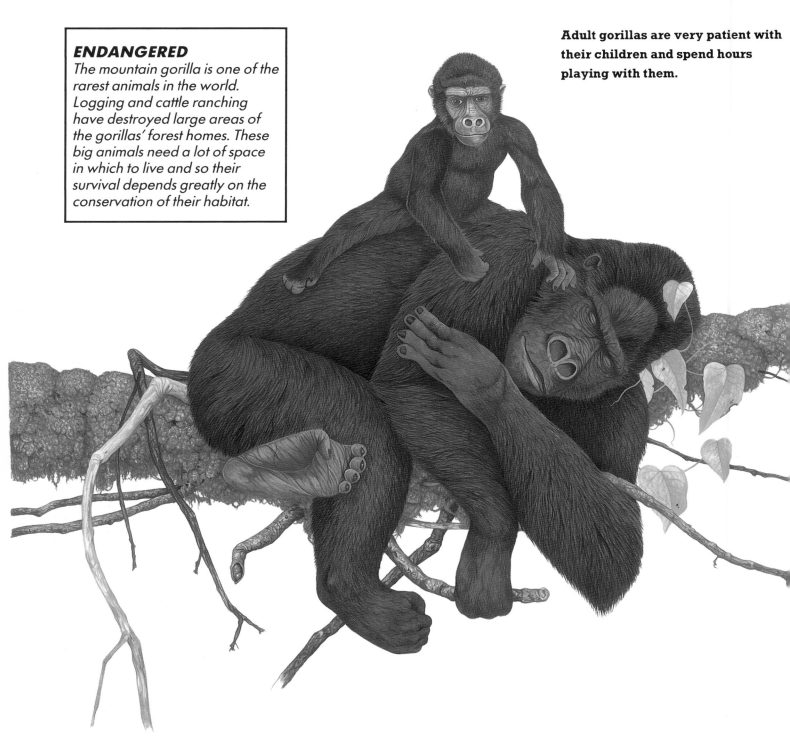

Despite its great strength, and impressive chest-beating displays, the gorilla is no more savage than any other wild animal. In fact, it is docile and friendly, and is only dangerous when threatened or harmed.

Gorillas are the largest of all apes. They can be taller than a man – and are often twice as heavy. Rare animals today, they live in small groups, or families, in the jungles of central Africa. Most of their time is spent on the ground, eating wild celery, roots, tree bark, and many other kinds of plant material. They do climb trees, usually to look for food or to get a bird's-eye view of their forest home. Sometimes they build sleeping nests there of branches and leaves.

They feed during the morning and evening but rest for a few hours at midday, when they love to sunbathe. Young gorillas spend a great deal of their time playing. They climb trees, slide down tree trunks, wrestle with each other, swing on branches, play chasing games, and even irritate the adults in the troop. Just like human children! But these playtimes are important in their growing up. They enable the young gorillas to copy what their parents do, and to learn how to climb, find food, and do other things.

Gorilla fact file:
There are three different kinds of gorilla: mountain, western lowland, and eastern lowland gorillas.

In some countries of Africa it is possible to visit gorilla families that allow people to sit with them while they eat.

Adult male gorillas are known as silverbacks because the hair on their backs turns from black to silver gray as they grow older.

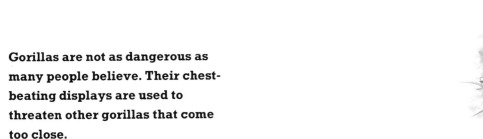

Gorillas are not as dangerous as many people believe. Their chest-beating displays are used to threaten other gorillas that come too close.

CONDOR

ENDANGERED

The California condor was hunted and poisoned for many years and is now a highly endangered species. By 1988 all California condors had been removed from the wild in the hope they could be bred in captivity and in this way saved from extinction. At that time there were only twenty-eight birds. By 1990, eighteen birds had been hatched and reared successfully in captivity.

The condor is an ugly bird on the ground, with no feathers on its face and a wrinkly flap of skin on its head.

The condor can survive for several weeks without eating. But when it finds food – usually a dead animal – it often eats so much that it cannot take off. The only solution is to walk up a nearby hill and jump into the air.

Like other members of the vulture family, a condor is an ugly bird on the ground, but in the air it is beautiful and graceful, able to soar effortlessly for hours without needing to flap its wings. With a wingspan of over nine feet, it is one of the largest flying birds in the world. One of its extinct relatives was even bigger, measuring twice as much from wingtip to wingtip.

There are two different kinds of condor. One lives in the Andes mountains of South America and the other is found in a small area of California. Both are uncommon, the California condor now so rare that it may soon become extinct.

Condors nest in cliff caves and inside hollow trees. They breed only once every two years, laying just one egg at a time. The newly hatched chick is carefully looked after by its parents for more than a year. It does not breed until it is at least seven years old.

Condor fact file:
A condor can glide for many miles without having to flap its wings.

Condors have long toes that give them a better grip when they are perched in a tree or on a rock.

Condors have excellent eyesight to help them find dead animals from high in the air.

In the air a condor is an impressively beautiful and graceful bird.

MOUNTAIN ANIMALS

Macaque fact file:
There are fifteen species of macaque, including the pig-tailed, lion-tailed, and crab-eating macaques.

Male macaques are always larger than the females.

The macaques' closest relatives are the baboons of Africa.

Some macaques have bright red faces.

On very cold days, Japanese macaques will spend hours and hours sitting in hot-spring water to keep warm.

Japanese macaques are astonishingly like people in many ways. They learn quickly and are able to teach one another different tricks and techniques. They are even able to walk on two legs, carrying their food in their arms as they go.

During bad winters, Japanese macaques keep themselves warm by taking regular hot baths. They have learned that the warm water from volcanic springs is ideal for sitting in, to keep out of the cold, and for protection from snowstorms. Only their heads stick out of the water, and these often get covered with snow that sometimes collects to several inches thick on top!

The only problem with taking baths is that the macaques have to climb out of the springs to search for food. The temperature outside is often well below freezing, and the snow can be several feet deep. The poor animals must get very cold, especially when their long and shaggy coats are soaking wet.

Japanese macaques are big monkeys. They live in very large troops. Up to seven hundred have been seen together. They live high in the mountains of Japan. Although they are excellent climbers, they spend most of their time on the ground, bathing or searching for fruit, leaves, insects, or small animals to eat. Some of them wash their food in water, others dip it in the sea because they like the salty taste.

MOUNTAIN ANIMALS

Japanese macaques love sweet potatoes and often carry them to the nearest water to wash them before eating.

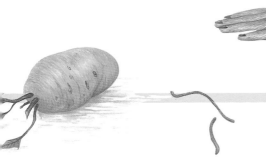

Snow geese   **Northern North America**

POLAR ANIMALS

The Arctic and the Antarctic are the coldest and windiest places on Earth. The Arctic is a sea surrounded by land, whereas the Antarctic is land surrounded by sea. Because both are covered with snow and ice for much of the year, they look quite similar.

Despite the harsh conditions, an incredible number of animals live around the two poles. The icy waters teem with tiny shrimplike creatures called krill that provide food for large numbers of seals, whales, fish, and seabirds. Many polar animals have special ways of coping with the extreme weather. They have thick fur, warm feathers, or extra layers of fat (called blubber) under their skin.

Snow geese are unusual because they have different colors in different parts of the world. Some are mainly white, others are mainly blue-gray.

The thick, woolly coat of the Arctic fox is white in winter and brown in summer.

The walrus uses its tusks to fight, to break through the Arctic ice, and to haul itself out of the water.

Adélie penguins are inquisitive birds that live along rocky coasts and islands in the Antarctic.

Killer whales are efficient hunters but they never kill for fun and rarely attack people.

**Arctic fox
Arctic tundra**

**Adélie penguin
Antarctic**

**Killer whale
Cool seas**

**Gyrfalcon
Arctic tundra**

**Arctic tern
Arctic**

**Weddell seal
Antarctic**

**Walrus
Arctic**

**Humpback whale
All seas**

The arctic tern lives near the coast
and feeds on fish and other small
sea animals.

The gyrfalcon, one of the largest
and most powerful of all the
falcons, lives in the cold sub-Arctic
and Arctic all year.

The Weddell seal lives in the
Antarctic and can dive to great
depths in the icy waters.

The humpback whale may weigh
more than fifty tons but it can still
leap clear out of the water.

NARWHAL

Narwhal fact file:
Unlike most whales and dolphins, the narwhal has no fin on its back.

Its closest living relative is another whale, called the beluga, which is pure white when fully grown.

Occasionally, a male narwhal has two tusks when both its teeth grow to an enormous size. A small number of females also grow tusks.

The narwhal has only two teeth. In the male and occasionally in the female, one of these grows so big that it sticks out through the upper lip and forms a spiraling tusk. Such tusks have been known to grow to nine feet in length.

No one really knows what the narwhal's tusk is for. It might be used to break through ice on the surface of the sea, to skewer prey, or to probe along the bottom of the sea for food. However, it is most likely to be used as a weapon. Narwhals have been seen using them like swords, fencing each other at the ocean surface. This may be quite common, as many of the animals have nasty scars, and one was even seen with a broken tusk sticking out of its head.

Narwhals are whales that live in the cold waters of the Arctic, particularly between northern Canada and Greenland. They feed on fish, shrimp, squid, octopuses, and other ocean animals. They are able to dive to depths of more than one thousand feet and to stay underwater for as long as fifteen minutes.

Narwhals probably use their long tusks as weapons for fighting and showing off in the same way that many deer use their antlers.

In the summer they often swim into shallow inlets called estuaries and fiords to have their young. Their calves, about one third the size of the parents when they are first born, will eventually grow to a length of twelve to fifteen feet.

The male narwhal is one of the most extraordinary animals living in the sea.

> ### *ENDANGERED*
> *The use of guns in narwhal hunting has resulted in a great decline in their numbers. For each narwhal that is caught, an estimated four more are shot but sink before they can be recovered. Eskimos hunt these unusual creatures for their meat and ivory tusks.*

EMPEROR PENGUIN

POLAR ANIMALS

Penguin fact file:
There are sixteen different species of penguin, ranging in size from the little blue penguin (twelve inches tall) to the enormous emperor.

Not all penguins live in the Antarctic. Some of them live in New Zealand, Australia, Africa, and South America. There is even one living in the Galapagos Islands, right on the Equator.

No penguins are able to fly, but all are expert swimmers and divers.

Emperor penguins can live for up to twenty years, but most penguins do not live longer than ten years.

The male emperor penguin looks after the egg for about two months while his mate is feeding at sea.

On land, penguins stand upright and waddle around on their short legs and webbed feet.

The emperor penguin has to put up with colder weather than almost any other bird in the world. At its breeding grounds in the Antarctic, temperatures drop to minus 50 degrees Fahrenheit. Strong winds blow up to fifty miles per hour. The penguins sometimes have to sit for days covered by snow.

The emperor is the largest of all penguins. Over three feet tall, it has waterproof, windproof feathers and a special layer of fat beneath its skin to keep warm.

Breeding colonies of emperor penguins are enormous. Each female lays a single egg in the very coldest month of the year, then leaves the male to keep it warm. As many as six thousand males may be left huddled together, each with an egg resting on his feet, protected from the cold outside world by a loose fold of skin from his belly hanging over it.

The males stay like this, without eating, for about two months. They take turns standing on the outside of the "rookery," where it is coldest, and they wait patiently for the females to return. Just as the eggs are about to hatch, the females appear. By this time the males are overtired and terribly thin.

Both parents feed the chicks, giving them large meals of fish and squid about once every three or four days. By the time the young are ready to leave the colony, the ice – which once separated them from the sea – has melted, and food, to keep them going until the following winter, has become plentiful again.

POLAR BEAR

A hungry polar bear will wait next to a hole in the ice for hours until an unsuspecting seal pops its head out of the water to breathe.

Bear fact file:

Bears live in many different habitats, from ice-bound coasts to tropical rain forests. They can be found in parts of the Arctic, North America, Europe, Asia, and South America.

There are seven different kinds of bear: polar, grizzly, American black, Asian black, spectacled, sun, and sloth bears.

Bears are large and powerful animals, but they can run very fast for short distances.

Polar bears love to have pretend fights, wrestling and pushing one another in play. Sliding down snowbanks on their bellies and swimming in the sea are other favorite pastimes. If they get bored or tired, they have a snooze until there is something else to do.

But these fun-loving animals are twice the size of a lion or tiger and considerably more powerful. A single swipe from one of their giant paws can kill a man. They can move with lightning speed and will eat almost anything they can catch or find. In some Alaskan and Canadian towns, they even raid garbage cans and rubbish heaps.

Seals, however, are their main food. The bears often sit quietly by a breathing hole in the ice, waiting to pounce the moment an unsuspecting seal comes up for air.

About twenty thousand polar bears live in the Arctic. Once there were many more, but they have been hunted for sport and money. These days the bears are protected and can safely travel all around their northern home. In fact, they can often be seen on pieces of floating ice hundreds or thousands of miles at sea.

Polar bear cubs are born in December and January in special snow dens. These consist of a tunnel, several feet long, leading to a "bedroom." The young bears spend the first few months of their lives in this room before venturing out for the first time.

ENDANGERED
In the first half of this century, polar bears were hunted for food, sport, and trade. Today the polar bear population appears to be stable but is still precariously low. The bears are protected by the Polar Bear Agreement which was signed in 1973. This allows only Eskimos and other traditional hunters to kill nearly a thousand bears every year.

Polar bears love to travel and will sometimes climb onto pieces of floating ice and wait patiently to see where they are being taken.

ARCTIC HARE

In winter, the arctic hare is completely white and blends in perfectly with its snowy surroundings.

The best way for an animal not to get eaten is to avoid being seen. This can be done by hiding or by blending in with its surroundings. The arctic hare is an expert at this form of hiding, called camouflage. Its colors are a kind of disguise that makes it difficult to be seen by wildcats, foxes, eagles, and other predators throughout the year.

As the seasons change the hare sheds its fur and grows a new coat. In summer it is brown and looks like any other hare, blending in perfectly with the browns and dark greens of the vegetation and soil. But in mid-October, as winter draws near, the color of its fur begins to change dramatically. By the time the first snows arrive it has turned completely white so that it blends in perfectly with the wintry surroundings.

Arctic hares have many different names, including mountain hare, snowshoe hare and blue hare. They are found in the northern and coldest parts of Europe and North America, coming out to feed – on heather and grass – between dusk and dawn. They sometimes graze in daylight as well, immediately before it rains or snows.

Young hares, called leverets, are born above ground with their eyes open and a full coat of fur. There are usually two in each litter, born at any time during the spring and summer. Many of the young die in the first few months of their lives, but the mothers usually have three litters every year.

Hare fact file:
There are twenty-one species of hare, found in a variety of habitats from the snow-covered Arctic to deserts.

Hares have long legs for running: Some of the larger ones can reach speeds of up to fifty miles per hour.

Hares are closely related to rabbits, but rabbits commonly live in burrows and most hares do not.

When they are born, young hares, or leverets, are covered with fur and their eyes are open. However, baby rabbits, called kittens, have no fur and their eyes do not open for several days.

SEA ANIMALS

The sea covers more than two thirds of the Earth's surface. It is divided into four main areas – the Pacific, Atlantic, Indian, and Arctic Oceans. There are also a number of smaller seas, such as the Caribbean and the Mediterranean. In some places, the water is so deep that Mount Everest could sit on the bottom and still be covered by more than half a mile of water.

It is home to some of the smallest animals in the world, called plankton, and also the largest animal that has ever existed, the blue whale. Hundreds of thousands of weird and wonderful creatures live in the sea, including the strange-looking angler fish, which lives in the cold and dark depths.

Galapagos penguin
Galapagos Islands

The Galapagos penguin is unusual because, unlike most penguins that live in the cold Antarctic, it lives on the Equator in the Galapagos Islands.

A flying fish can glide for nearly a quarter of a mile out of the water before falling back into the sea.

Common dolphins are intelligent and friendly animals that like living in large groups or "schools."

The weedy sea dragon is a sea horse found around the coast of Australia. It disguises itself as a piece of seaweed.

Weedy sea dragon
Coastal Australia

Flying fish
Cool and warm seas worldwide

Common dolphin
North Atlantic

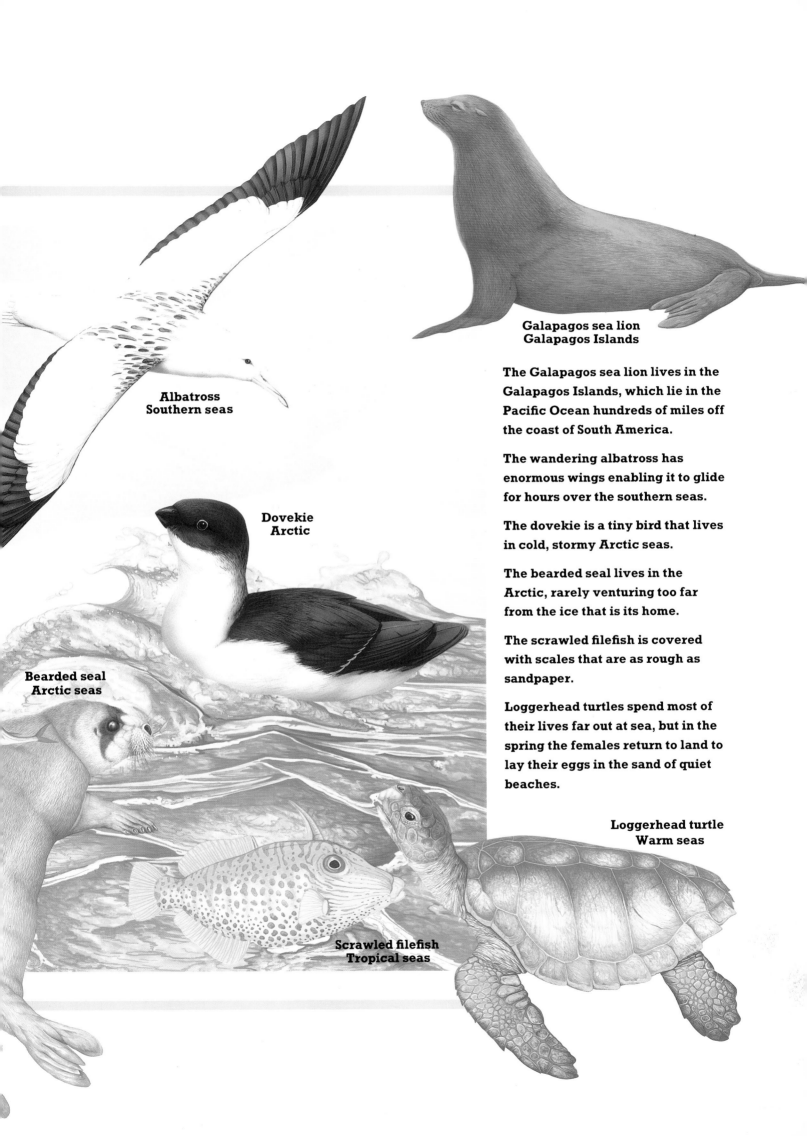

Albatross
Southern seas

Dovekie
Arctic

Bearded seal
Arctic seas

Scrawled filefish
Tropical seas

Galapagos sea lion
Galapagos Islands

The Galapagos sea lion lives in the
Galapagos Islands, which lie in the
Pacific Ocean hundreds of miles off
the coast of South America.

The wandering albatross has
enormous wings enabling it to glide
for hours over the southern seas.

The dovekie is a tiny bird that lives
in cold, stormy Arctic seas.

The bearded seal lives in the
Arctic, rarely venturing too far
from the ice that is its home.

The scrawled filefish is covered
with scales that are as rough as
sandpaper.

Loggerhead turtles spend most of
their lives far out at sea, but in the
spring the females return to land to
lay their eggs in the sand of quiet
beaches.

Loggerhead turtle
Warm seas

MARINE IGUANA

Iguana fact file:
There are six hundred and fifty different kinds of iguana.

Iguanas are found mainly in North, Central, and South America; but there are also some kinds in Madagascar, Fiji, and Tonga.

Most iguanas lay eggs, but a few species bear live young.

Iguanas love the sun and some can survive temperatures as high as 110 degrees F for short periods.

The head of a marine iguana, covered with bumps and scales, is quite ugly.

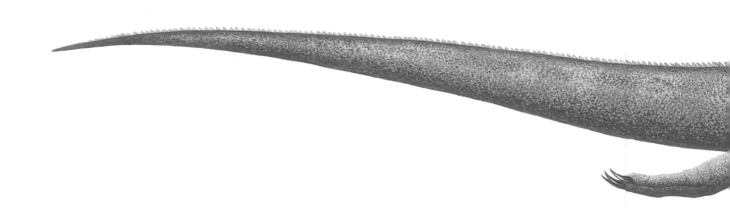

Along the beautiful shores of the Galapagos Islands, many miles off the coast of South America, thousands of giant lizards sunbathe on the rocks. Called marine iguanas, they spend every day warming themselves in the sun.

Although as much as three feet long, they are completely harmless creatures, feeding on seaweed and other water plants. They are the only lizards in the world that like to live in the sea.

The iguanas hide in rock crevices during the night, but they come out as soon as the sun begins to rise. When they have warmed up, they dive into the sea to find something to eat. They swim happily underwater, moving with a snakelike motion rather than paddling their legs. Occasionally they haul themselves onto a rock, clinging to it against the strength of the waves with their long, powerful claws.

During the breeding season, male iguanas often fight over females. They butt their heads together and try to push one another out of the way. But for the rest of the year they seem to be the best of friends, sunbathing side by side, even lying on top of one another.

The marine iguana swims underwater with a wriggling side-to-side motion, like a snake.

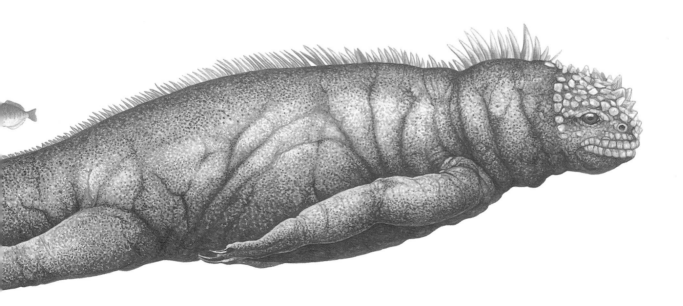

CALIFORNIA SEA LION

Sea lion fact file:
There are five different kinds of sea lion: California, Australian, South American, the New Zealand, and Steller's.

Male sea lions are always much larger than the females.

Sea lions like the company of other sea lions, and prefer not to be alone.

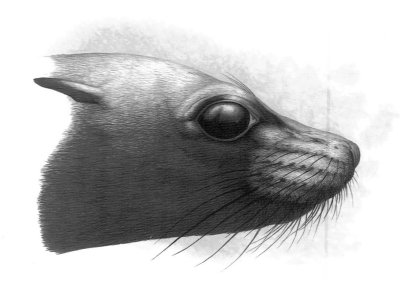

When they are on land, sea lions like to scratch themselves with their hind flippers.

California sea lions are so playful that sometimes they chase and catch their own air bubbles underwater. They are also very intelligent and have a good memory, making them popular circus animals. Indeed, they are probably best known for balancing balls on their noses, clapping with their flippers, and blowing circus trumpets.

In the wild, they often play together by leaping from the water and diving back in headfirst. Groups of up to twenty young sea lions will swim along in single file to perform this favorite trick one after the other.

Several species of sea lion live in many parts of the world, but the California sea lion, about eight feet long, is found only in the Pacific Ocean. It lives along the coast and islands of western North America, particularly California and Mexico. It also occurs farther south, in the Galapagos Islands, where it is known as the Galapagos sea lion.

Sea lions hunt at any time of day or night, mostly for squid and octopuses. They also feed on a variety of fish, including herring, sardines, hake, and rockfish. Sleek and graceful in the water, they are fast and efficient hunters. But they are hunted themselves by people and frequently also have to use their swimming skills to avoid such enemies as killer whales and sharks.

Sea lions and seals have excellent hearing and can detect sounds both underwater and above the surface. But not all have obvious external ears. Many have only tiny holes in the sides of their heads. The California sea lion, however, is one of the exceptions and does have small ears that can be seen.

California sea lions love to chase their own air bubbles under the water.

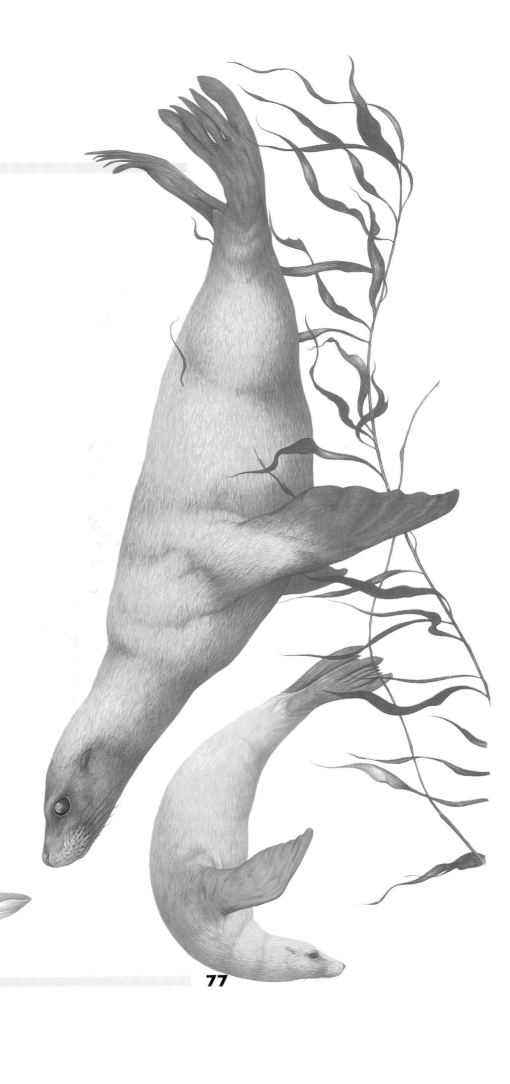

SHARK

Sharks are probably the most feared animals in the world. With their streamlined bodies, needle-sharp teeth, glaring eyes, and noses that can smell food from miles away, they have a terrible reputation.

But not all sharks are dangerous. Some are barely six inches long, and are incapable of causing much harm. Two of the world's biggest – the forty-foot whale shark and the thirty-foot basking shark – eat tiny animals called plankton and are completely harmless. Most other kinds eat fish. Even the so-called man-eating sharks often swim past people without attacking.

Shark fact file:

There are nearly three hundred and fifty species of shark living in the world's oceans.

Almost all sharks live in salt water, although some occasionally venture into freshwater rivers.

Shark tails differ in size and shape according to the habits of the species.

Sharks are always breaking their teeth, but they have spare ones ready to move into position as soon as they are needed.

But it is true that some, like the hammerhead and great white sharks, can be very dangerous. To a twenty-foot great white shark, with teeth the length of a finger, a fully grown person would make a tasty snack.

No one knows for sure how often these and other sharks injure or kill people. About fifty attacks are reported from around the world every year; as many as a thousand more probably go unrecorded. Even so, the chances of any one person actually being attacked – or even seeing a shark – while swimming in the sea are very small indeed.

Sharks come in a variety of different shapes and sizes and not all of them are dangerous.

BLUE WHALE

The blue whale is so large that even its calf weighs more than an elephant when it is first born.

The blue whale is the largest animal that has ever lived. Weighing more than two hundred tons and measuring up to one hundred feet long, a blue whale is even bigger than the largest of all the dinosaurs. Even baby blue whales are about twenty feet long and weigh as much as eight tons when they are first born. They drink six hundred quarts of their mother's milk every day and often double their weight in a week.

Blue whales, now very rare, are found in all the world's oceans. During this century alone, at least 350,000 have been killed by people for their meat and oil. The blue whale has been protected since 1966, but the species is so seriously endangered that the population is still only a few thousand.

Whale fact file:

There are seventy-six different species of whales, dolphins, and porpoises living in oceans and some rivers.

Unlike sharks, whales are warm-blooded animals, and they breathe air with lungs rather than through gills.

Most of the larger whales, such as the blue whale, do not have teeth, but use a special filtering system to catch their food.

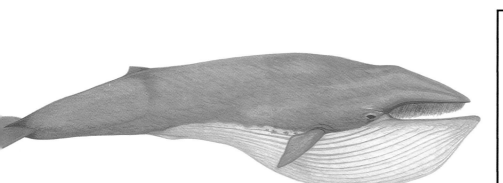

ENDANGERED

The blue whale was once extensively hunted as a source of meat and oil. From 1930 to 1931 — just one year — an incredible 30,000 blue whales were killed. The population has never recovered. Blue whales became so rare that it was difficult for whalers to make hunting profitable. Whalers turned their attention to other great whales. Hunting blue whales was banned in 1965, but by then this magnificent creature was already close to extinction.

Despite their enormous size, blue whales feed entirely on tiny shrimplike animals called krill. Some krill are less than one inch long, and so the whales have to eat enormous numbers, probably as many as four million every day. But they only feed during the summer months, preferring not to eat at all for about eight months of the year.

Blue whales are mammals, not fish, and so they have to come to the surface to breathe about every quarter hour. For this reason they cannot stay underwater or sleep for too long, otherwise they would drown. When they rise to the surface, they breathe out through their blowholes, spouting water over thirty feet into the air, before breathing in and diving once again.

The blue whale feeds by swimming with its mouth open into large shoals of tiny shrimplike animals called krill.

SEA OTTER

ENDANGERED

Sea otters were once endangered because of hunting for their valuable fur. Fortunately, they have been legally protected since 1911. Many sea otters today live in reserves. Their survival may still be threatened due mainly to oil pollution. They can easily die of cold if their fur becomes oil-soaked and can no longer provide insulation.

Sea otters use their tails and hind legs for swimming, leaving the front legs free to search for and carry food.

Sea otters often sleep with their paws over their eyes. Lying in the water, they may also tie themselves to giant seaweed to avoid drifting out to sea during the night.

They spend most of their lives in the water, though never so far out that they lose sight of land. The only times they climb out of the water are during particularly bad storms.

Sea otters live along the rocky coasts of the North Pacific in western North America and eastern Russia. They are excellent swimmers, paddling along with their hind legs and using their tails as oars. They can dive to depths of more than one hundred feet. On the sea bed, they search for crabs, mussels, fish, snails, sea urchins, and other animals, catching the prey with their front paws. They then swim to the surface to eat, cracking open the shells with a stone and using their chests as tables while floating on their backs. When they have finished, they simply roll over to wash the bits of shell and leftover food from their fur.

Sometimes sea otters use stones to crack open shells to get at the tasty animals inside.

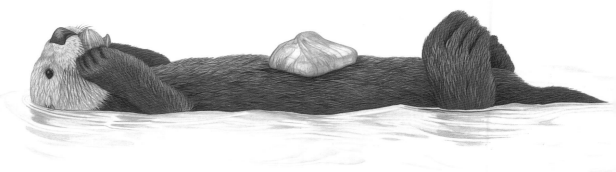

Baby otters are born in the water and ride on their mothers' chests for six or seven weeks. Then they begin taking lessons in swimming, diving, and catching food. These last for as long as six months, until the babies are able to look after themselves.

Otter fact file:
There are thirteen different species of otter, ranging from the tiny oriental short-clawed otter, which is little more than one and a half feet long, to the enormous giant otter that, including its tail, can be nearly six feet long.

Otters belong to the weasel family, hence are closely related to weasels, ferrets, mink, skunks, and badgers.

Otters are very noisy animals and will often call, twitter, and chuckle to one another.

Sea otters spend the night safely wrapped up in giant seaweed.

DESERT ANIMALS

Deserts are the driest places on Earth. Some may go for months or even years without rain. But even desert animals cannot survive without water or for long periods in the scorching sun. They have different ways of coping with the harsh conditions. Gerbils, for example, spend the hottest part of the day in cool underground burrows. Darkling beetles are experts at catching drops of moisture on their legs, then lifting them into the air until the drops trickle down into their mouths.

Not all deserts are endless seas of rolling sand. Some are rocky or pebbly and dotted with small bushes; others are sprinkled with colorful flowers during the spring.

Elf owl
Mexico and Southwestern U.S.

The elf owl often nests inside giant cacti and feeds its young large insects.

The Arabian oryx became extinct in the wild in 1972. But oryx bred in captivity are gradually being returned to their old desert homes in several parts of Arabia.

The ostrich is the largest bird in the world. It may stand nearly nine feet tall.

Ostrich
Africa

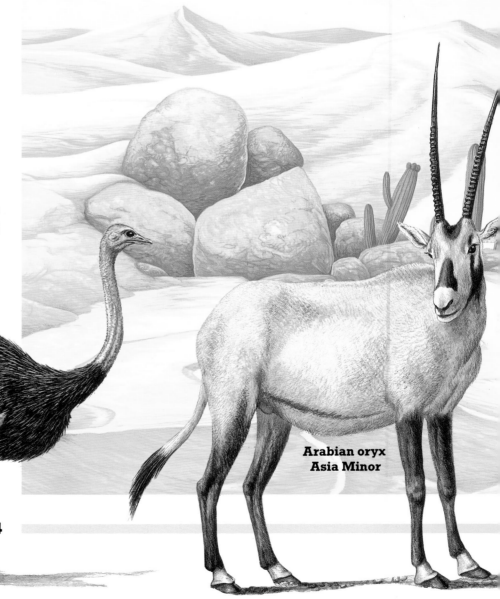

Arabian oryx
Asia Minor

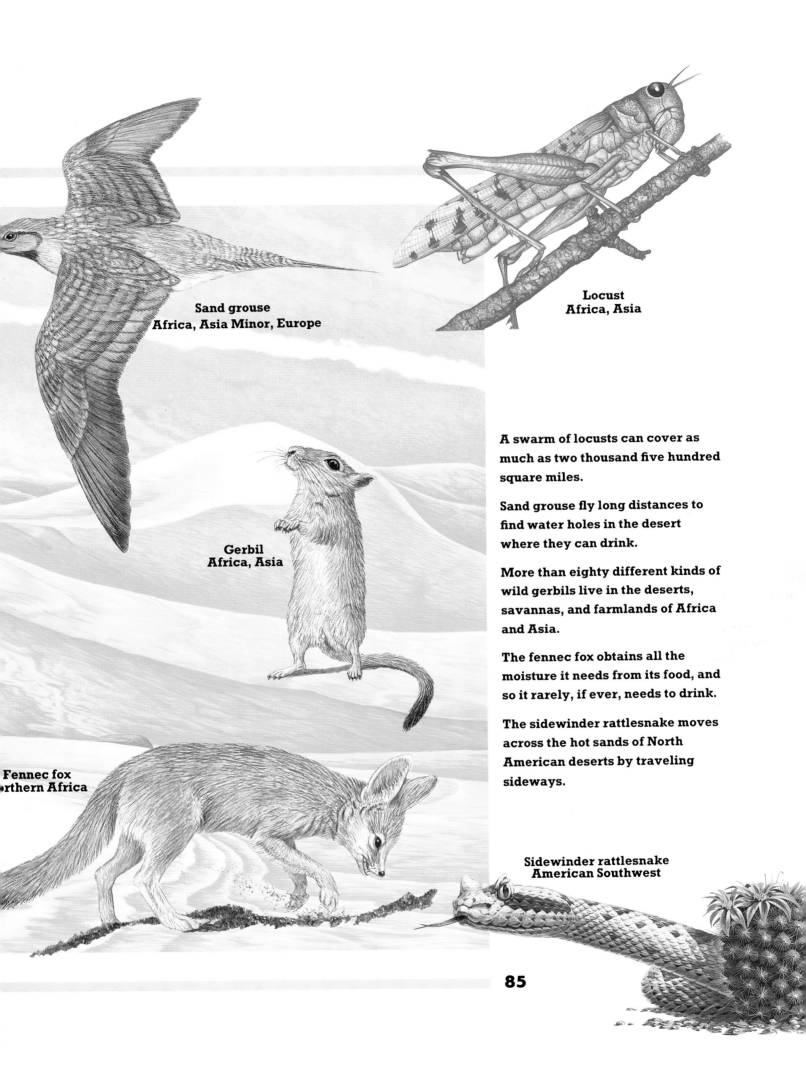

Sand grouse
Africa, Asia Minor, Europe

Locust
Africa, Asia

Gerbil
Africa, Asia

Fennec fox
rthern Africa

A swarm of locusts can cover as much as two thousand five hundred square miles.

Sand grouse fly long distances to find water holes in the desert where they can drink.

More than eighty different kinds of wild gerbils live in the deserts, savannas, and farmlands of Africa and Asia.

The fennec fox obtains all the moisture it needs from its food, and so it rarely, if ever, needs to drink.

The sidewinder rattlesnake moves across the hot sands of North American deserts by traveling sideways.

Sidewinder rattlesnake
American Southwest

RATTLESNAKE

Snake fact file:
There are more than two thousand three hundred different kinds of snakes around the world, ranging from just six inches long to more than thirty feet.

Most snakes are quite harmless, but a few are so poisonous that they can kill a person with a single bite.

Most snakes lay eggs, but some give birth to live young.

In the dry, rocky deserts of America lives an evil-looking snake with a very bad reputation.

Its buzzing rattle can be heard one hundred feet away, and it can strike with lightning speed.

But the rattlesnake prefers to avoid people if it possibly can. It holds its tail upright and rattles the end whenever it is disturbed. If this warning is ignored – and it feels threatened – the snake will strike at an intruder.

The rattler itself cannot hear the noise its tail makes. Like most snakes, it detects vibrations in the ground. When a person walks nearby, the snake can feel the movement, but if the same person shouts, the snake would not hear a thing.

Rattlesnakes are widespread on the American continents from Canada to Argentina. They feed on a variety of prey, including mice, voles, rats, chipmunks, and many other small animals. Young rattlers are born alive and can be up to one third of the length of their parents.

Rattlesnakes kill their prey with venom. Like all snakes, they swallow animals whole. Few snakes eat more than once a week. Some, like the larger pythons, can survive for a year or more without eating.

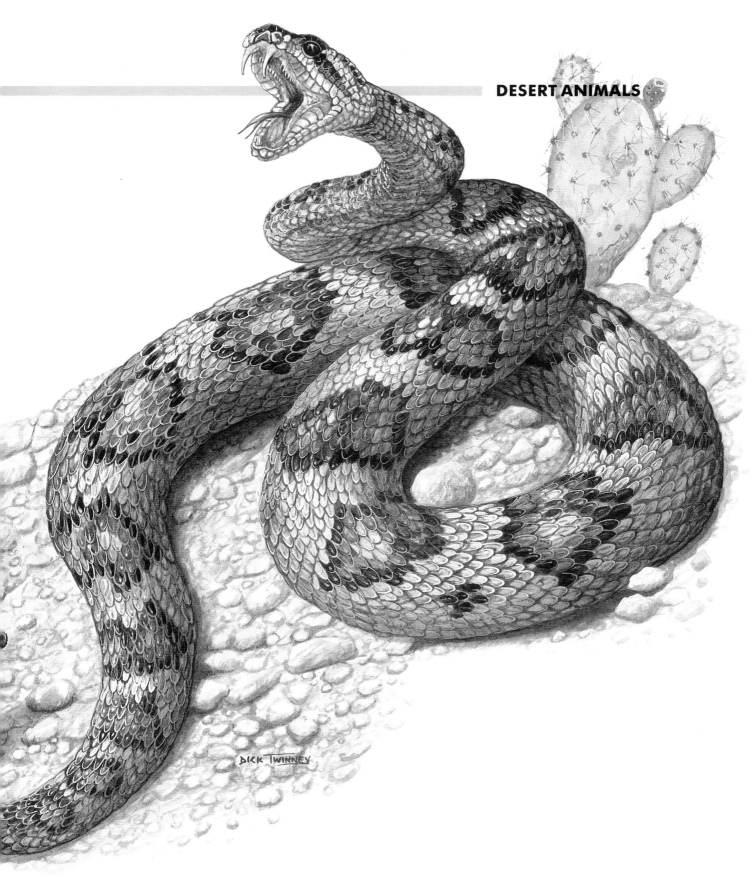

SCORPION

Baby scorpions ride on their mothers' backs until they are old enough to take care of themselves.

Scorpions rank among the least popular of all desert animals. They are common in most deserts, but they hide under rocks or debris and are rarely seen.

They come out at night, when the desert is cooler, to hunt for beetles, cockroaches, and other small animals. The size of the prey depends on the size of the scorpion, and large scorpions may be as much as seven inches long.

Once it has caught an animal with its pincerlike front legs – especially if the animal tries to struggle free – the scorpion stings it with the needlelike tip of its tail. This sting is used also in self-defense. It feels like a very fast and painful injection, which can either paralyze or kill. In most cases, however, it is no more serious than a bee sting. A few of the twelve hundred species of scorpions in the world are deadly, however. The poison of the Sahara scorpion is as strong as the venom of a cobra and can kill a dog within seconds.

Scorpions are related to spiders. Like their long-legged relatives, they often have impressive courtship displays. The male holds his mate's pincers and walks her round and round in circles. This is called the "scorpion's dance."

The female lays eggs that hatch almost immediately into miniature scorpions. They are smaller versions of their parents. The babies climb onto their mothers' back, and are carried by, her wherever she goes until they are old enough to take care of themselves.

Scorpion fact file:
Scorpions are ideally suited to desert life because they can survive great heat.

A scorpion will use the sting on the end of its tail only if its prey is very large or tries to struggle free.

Scorpions do not like the company of other scorpions and prefer to live alone.

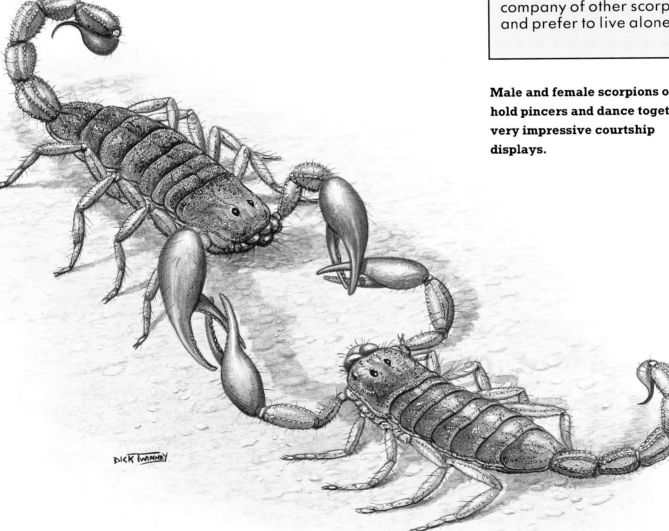

Male and female scorpions often hold pincers and dance together in very impressive courtship displays.

BANDED MONGOOS

Mongooses like to hunt together, but they always keep a lookout for dangerous predators.

Poking their noses into holes, overturning rocks with their paws, and scratching the ground with their sharp claws, banded mongooses are amusing animals to watch. A common sight in many parts of Africa, they travel in groups of about twenty to forage for beetles, millipedes, and other small, tasty creatures.

They like to hunt together, keeping in touch whenever out of sight, behind rocks or bushes, by twittering and calling. Always on the lookout for danger – such as hawks, eagles, and large snakes – they warn one another with a special alarm call if they see anything suspicious.

Mongooses are famous for being able to kill snakes without getting hurt themselves. Their reactions are so fast that they can dodge each time the snake strikes. They continually make a nuisance of themselves until, after a while, when the snake gets tired, they dive in quickly for the kill.

DICK TWIHNEY

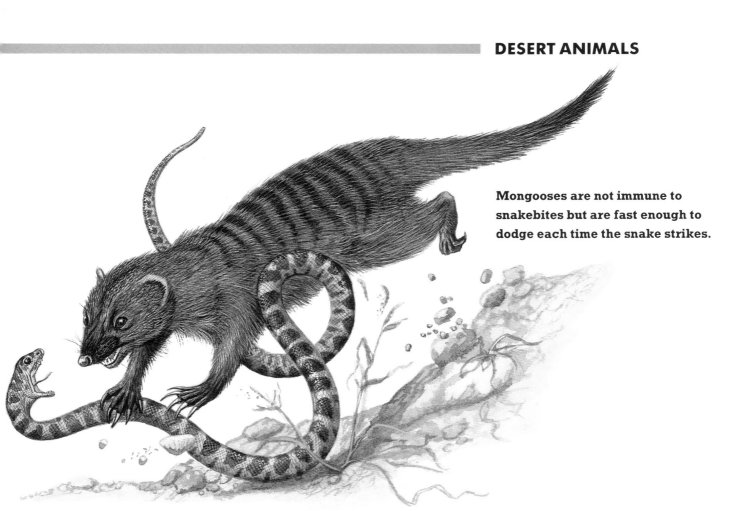

Mongooses are not immune to snakebites but are fast enough to dodge each time the snake strikes.

All the females have their kittens at about the same time. They are raised by the whole group in a den made inside an old termite mound or a hollow log. When most of the adults are out looking for food, one or two males stay behind to stand guard until the others return for the night.

Mongoose fact file:
There are thirty-one species of mongoose in southern Europe, Africa, and parts of Asia.

Mongooses often make their dens inside termite mounds.

Mongooses sometimes travel long distances – up to six miles or more in a day – in search of food.

CAMEL

Camel fact file:

Camels are closely related to llamas and alpacas.

Camels were first domesticated as beasts of burden many thousands of years ago.

In the wild, camels usually live in small groups of up to thirty animals.

Camels have long, shaggy winter coats to keep warm, and shorter, tidier coats in the summer to keep cool.

A thirsty camel can drink as much as thirty gallons of water – that's about five hundred full glasses – in just ten minutes. Normally, however, it gets all the moisture it needs from desert plants and can survive for up to ten months without drinking any water at all.

There are two different kinds of camel. One, known as the dromedary, or Arabian, has only a single hump. The other, called a Bactrian camel, has two humps. The humps help the animals to survive in the desert, by acting as storage containers. They don't store water – as many people wrongly believe. Rather, they are full of fat. This fat nourishes the camel when food is scarce. If they have nothing to eat for several days, their humps shrink as the fat is used up.

There are many other ways in which camels are adapted to desert life. Their mouths are so tough that even the sharp thorns

Baby camels do not grow to full size until they are at least five years old.

of desert plants don't hurt them. They can survive at much higher temperatures than most other animals. They even have bushy eyebrows and a double row of eyelashes to keep out the desert sand.

There are many millions of camels throughout the world, but they have nearly all been domesticated, or tamed, by man. Probably fewer than a thousand are now left roaming in the wild.

Camels are better adapted to living in the desert than almost any other animal.

DICK TWINNEY

AUSTRALIAN FRILLE

Lizard fact file:
There are over three thousand seven hundred and fifty different kinds of lizard around the world, ranging in size from less than an inch long to more than nine feet long.

The lizard family includes chameleons, iguanas, geckos, and monitors.

Many lizards are able to lose their tails to escape the grasp of a predator. Eventually, they are able to grow new tails.

Most lizards run away or hide when they are frightened or under attack, but the Australian frilled lizard stands firm and tries to scare its enemies away. It opens a gigantic flap of loose skin, called a ruff, behind its head and inflates its body. This makes it look much bigger – and much more dangerous – than it actually is. Then it makes horrible and furious hissing sounds like a snake.

Normally, the sight of a frilled lizard in action is enough to frighten off even the boldest and biggest of its enemies. But if the ruff, which can be as much as twelve inches across, doesn't scare off the enemy, the lizard runs away, speeding off on its hind legs.

Frilled lizards are also able to climb trees. They often leave the desert floor in their constant search for insects, spiders, and other small animals suitable for eating.

Found in northern Australia and New Guinea, they can grow to more than two and one half feet long. They usually keep their ruffs folded back against their bodies, almost out of sight, unless an enemy comes near, but they use them also for court-ship in a spectacular display to impress potential mates.

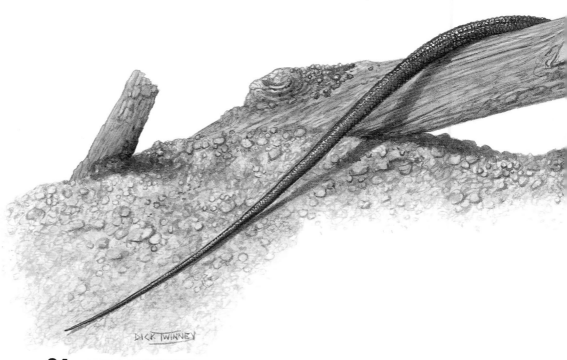

ZARD

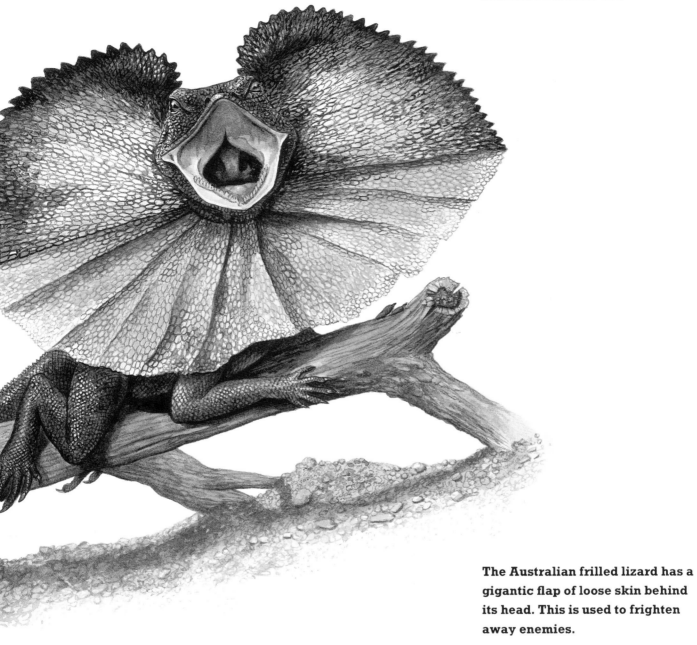

The Australian frilled lizard has a gigantic flap of loose skin behind its head. This is used to frighten away enemies.

INDEX

A
aardvark, 48–49
albatross, 73
aye-aye, 8–9

B
badger, 22–23
bear
    brown, 19
    polar, 68–69
beaver, 30
bush baby, 26–27

C
camel, 92–93
cat
    fishing, 32–33
    polecat, 19
chamois, 53
chimpanzee, 44–45
chinchilla, 53
chipmunk, 18
condor, 58–59
cougar, 53
crocodile, 31

D
dolphin
    Amazon River, 10–11
    common, 72
duckbilled platypus, 31
duck, torrent, 40–41

E
egret, cattle, 42

F
fish
    flying, 72
    scrawled filefish, 73
fox
    arctic, 62
    bat-eared, 50–51
    fennec, 85
    red, 18
frog, goliath, 31

G
gavial, 34–35
genet, 20–21
gerbil, 85
gibbon, 7
giraffe, 43
goose, snow, 62
gorilla, 56–57
gyrfalcon, 63

H
hare, arctic, 70–71
hippopotamus, 36–37
hyena, spotted, 46–47

I
ibex, Spanish, 52
iguana, marine, 74–75

J
jaguar, 7

K
kangaroo, 43
kingfisher, 30
koala, 19

L
lemur, ring-tailed, 24–25
leopard, snow, 54–55
lion, 43
lizard, Australian frilled, 94–95
llama, 53
locust, 85

M
macaque, Japanese, 60–61
manatee, 31
mongoose, banded, 90–91
monkey
    golden lion tamarin, 7
    howler, 12–13
    proboscis, 6
moose, 38–39
mouse, harvest, 42
mynah bird, 19

N
narwhal, 64–65

O
oryx, Arabian, 84
ostrich, 84
otter, 30
    sea, 82–83
owl
    barn, 28–29
    elf, 84

P
panda, giant, 52
pelican, white, 31
penguin
    adélie, 62
    emperor, 66–67
    Galapagos, 72
pika, 52
polecat, 19
prairie dog, 42

Q
quelea, red-billed, 43
quetzal, 6

R
rabbit, volcano, 52
raccoon, 18
rattlesnake, 86–87
rhinoceros, black, 42

S
salmon, Atlantic, 30
sand grouse, 85
scorpion, 88–89
sea dragon, 72
sea lion
    California, 76–77
    Galapagos, 73
seal
    bearded, 72
    Weddell, 63
shark, 78–79
sidewinder, 85
sloth, 14–15
squirrel
    flying, 19
    red, 18

T
tapir, Malayan, 16–17
tern, arctic, 63
toucan, 6
turtle, loggerhead, 73

V
vampire bat, 7
vulture, 43

W
walrus, 63
whale
    blue, 80–81
    humpback, 63
    killer, 62
woodpecker, 18

Y
yak, 53

Z
zebra, 42